COP KILLAS, JUSTICE SERVED D. MANN

I0654477

This book is the fictional work of the author. Any semblance to any actuality is merely coincidence. All opinions expressed are solely those of the author.

Copyright © 2015 by D. Mann

All rights reserved. No part of this publication may be reproduced, stored in or introduced into a retrieval system, or transmitted, in any form, or by any means (electronic, mechanical, photocopying, recording, or otherwise), without the prior written permission of both the copyright owner and the above publisher of this book.

ISBN: 978-0-9966466-2-8

Edited by N. Miller

Cover Design by Black Lyfe Publications

COP

KILLAS

By D. Mann

Chapter 1

First Served

Darryl Arrington was awaken by the screams in his head. It was a horror that he recounted on an almost a nightly basis. This wasn't a dream though, it was his reality. Cold sweats were such a regular occurrence that DA (as he was known in the streets) kept a folded towel on the night stand next to his bed.

It was nineteen years ago to the day when the vivid memories of death started to haunt the then six year old. Now at the age of twenty five, DA would put those bad memories to rest once and for all.

DA sat up in his bed, drenched in sweat. He grabbed the towel off the nightstand and began wiping himself dry. He grabbed the remote and turned on his flat screen television. DA would use the sounds of the television to drown out the screams in his head.

DA looked at the time on the television, it read 2:45 a.m. He began wiping his face again but this time DA was wiping away his tears. He had been crying those tears for the last nineteen years.

COP KILLAS, JUSTICE SERVED D. MANN

DA climbed out of the bed and headed for the bathroom. The splashes of warm water to his face and a deep breath was just the temporary relief that he needed.

DA stared at himself through the mirror, penetrating his own soul until the words *it's time* sounded off in his mind.

DA got dressed, grabbed his small gym bag and headed downstairs to the garage. He pulled his 2013 Black Suburban out of the garage and guided it down the rain slicken streets. This was an early morning appointment that had been in the making for most of his life; DA wouldn't miss it to save his own.

The heavy rain and early morning hours had the streets quiet as a cemetery. DA pulled over and parked. He reach in his glove box and retrieved a small bottle of Hennessey. Guzzling down the alcohol, DA reclined his seat back and lit himself a cigarette.

DA took his time slowly, only taking a few puffs of the cigarette before putting it out. "Time to pay the piper," He murmured, pulling his hoodie over his head and stepping out the truck.

Chapter 2

Meet & Greet

Retired Police Officer John Smith poured himself a glass of milk and walked into the living room to watch the early morning news. He pushed the on button on the side of the television, grabbed the remote and started flickering through the channels as he made the familiar walk backwards to his chair.

He sat his glass of milk on a table next to the chair. Channel seven was the only station airing the news this early so he left it on that channel and began taking a seat.

"What the fuck?" John screeched, quickly bouncing away and spinning around to take sight of a man holding a nine millimeter with a silencer.

"Who the fuck are you? And what the fuck you doing in my house?" John screamed. "You making a big mistake here. You know who I am son?" John said.

"Yeah. I know who you are Officer John. Your big mistake is the reason that I'm here," The man answered, rising from the chair. "My name is Darryl Arrington Jr. Does that ring an old bell?"

5

"Arrington! I don't know any got damn Arring…" John uttered, before pausing.

"I see your recollection is still good," DA said, calmly tossing the retired officer a pair of handcuffs. "Hook yourself behind the back. See how well you remember that routine."

John complied locking his hands behind his back. "Now what?"

DA checked the cuffs, tightening them around the retired cop's wrist until he grunted.

"Have a seat," DA answered, placing the pistol on the table.

Both men sat quietly for a second eyeing one another intently. DA's stare was filled with resolve while Officer John's eyes showed a plea for mercy. John knew what was going on.

"I'll tell you whatever you wanna know. Just don't kill me," John begged, looking as sorrowful as possible.

"Tell me something I don't know," DA murmured, in a low tone retrieving his bag from behind the chair. "Other than that, I stay on course."

John hung his head low and began shaking it from side-to-side. He looked up to see DA withdraw a military style Rambo knife with the jagged edges on top, out of the bag.

DA walked over to John and let the tip of the blade swing downward stopping at John's groin area. As soon as John felt the tip of the blade brush against his boxers, his body jumped and he started singing like an opera.

DA listened closely while he removed the knife from John's boxers. DA took a seat again and began pulling more instruments from his bag placing them on the table.

"You even think of lying to me Officer John and I'll draw more blood outta yo' ass than a new med school student," DA warned, quickly glancing up at John as if he was close to speaking an untruth.

DA was far from naïve, he knew the cop would try to absolve himself of guilt while incriminating everyone else. It was the typical coward's move. DA wasn't here to hold trial though, he was here exact sentencing…the death penalty!

John ran his lips faster than a short distance runner, he was telling things that DA had no knowledge of. DA had to force an extra control of himself when John mentioned certain incidents. DA was boiling hot.

"I remember some nineteen years ago, you taking a delight in torturing my uncle Officer John," DA recalled, sneaking a peek from the top of the staircase. "It seems that you were more than happy to show the white cops you were a team player."

"Those white cops would have killed me if I hadn't done what they told me to do," John argued. "I didn't have a choice."

"Now now John. Sure you did. And here's the choice I'm giving you now, even though you playing the helpless victim card." DA issued. "Give me the addresses of every cop that was there with you that night, the shot caller of your unit and you'll survive with a well whooped ass. If you don't, you'll be hanging from your vaulted living room when they find your body."

DA already had the current addresses for three other officers, he wanted to know who pulled the strings. This was nothing more than a ploy. DA knew John would never divulge any true information involving his colleagues.

John was a loyal German shepherd to his masters, always so willing and eager to please. This plan wasn't about information, it was about testing his loyalty to known racists. Would John give them up or would he lie to save them?

"Who's the master that was pulling your leash John?" DA asked, glaring intently into the eyes of the pitiful looking John.

DA listened carefully as John told lie after lie trying to escape his fate.

DA's face never showed it but his anger was starting to arise. *Let this muthafucka insult my intelligence one more time. He not even a good liar*, DA thought to himself as he pulled a rope from his bag and slowly started forming the rope into a noose.

John eyes grew big as silver dollars when he saw DA fashioning the rope into a noose. He became silent.

"Continue on," DA spoke, still working the rope. "Don't stop on my account."

"You plan on hanging me! I thought you said you wouldn't kill me," John cried out.

"I lied," DA answered. "Just like you did."

"I didn't lie. I told you the truth," Officer John implored.

John's pleas fell on death ears. DA was no longer listening to his cries. DA walked over to John, placed the rope around his neck and tightened it loosely.

"What kind of black man lynches another black man?" John questioned.

"The kind of black man that hates house niggas," DA replied. "You were willing to die for them. Well this is how they kill us, then and now."

"Brother I was just doing my job," John spoke, pleading for his life.

"You should've resigned" DA interrupted. "Since you didn't I'm here to terminate your retirement."

"Please don't kill me. We can work something out," John cried. "I was a black cop. I protected the hood from the criminals."

"A BLACK COP! Let me tell you a story about you black cops," DA said, dropping the rope and walking to the dining room table.

DA came back with a chair placing it directly under the ceiling vaults and continued with his story.

"It took me a long time to understand why black cops sat around passively while white cops abuse and killed our people, their people. Then it hit me, they stay silent to keep that itty bitty piece of privilege called power of authority," DA spoke sternly. "The sad thing is, it's not a power that allows y'all to check y'all colleagues for their wrong doing but it is a power that allows y'all, to whoop black asses that look just like you…for white peer acceptance. Y'all love the praises of a white man."

John glanced upward catching DA's stare. John's spirit had heard the truth, his head sunk low. DA continued his speech.

"See the way I see it, every time one of you black cop puts on his or her uniform you denounce your identity. You're not a black man, you're a cop. You're not a black cop, you're just a cop," DA emphasized, pounding both fist up and down in the air. "It's no such thing as a black cop! A black cop could never survive in a white racist department such as the police, without selling out."

John's head raised again. He met DA's disapproving eyes. John's head sunk low again. DA continued his speech.

"They're normally silent and condoning of the actions or they're house niggas like you," DA uttered.

John didn't peek upward at hearing that comment and DA continued his speech.

"I bet not one you so-called black cops has ever stopped a white cop from killing a black person," DA growled. "And you so-called black cops in

America barely ever kill a white person. If they do, the white boy must be super criminal cause' we all know ain't no black cops around here, killing no innocent unarmed white boys. Why is that?"

"I don't know," John answered, in a low whimper.

"Because you house niggas know better, that's why. White America would burn yo' ass on a cross," DA barked, grabbing the rope and tossing it over the vault.

A flashback in his mind provided the clarity of a telescope. It was brewing his anger again. It was like watching a clear copy of the worst day of his life over and over.

"Not to mention that it would piss yo' master off," DA stated.

DA began pulling the rope downwards, causing the rope to partially choke the officer. DA stretched his body far upwards as he could, yanking the rope in one big gesture. The tug had so much energy to it, it drug John to his knees crashing his forehead against the hard wood floors.

The rope had tightened enough to kill off any attempted cries for help. John squirmed like a fish out of water gasping at every breath of oxygen available to his lungs. "Huuh-huuh-huuh."

"On yo' feet John," DA called out, helping the desperate John to his feet. John's watering eyes pronounced every plea mentionable.

DA's eyes returned a callous *I don't give a fuck* look.

"If memory serves me well I recall your last words to my uncle being something like," DA paused, taking a second for thought. "Umm stop being a bitch, take it like a man right?"

"Up," DA demanded, pulling the rope more and ushering John to the top of the chair.

John tried to speak but the noose was too tight.

"Here let me help you," DA said, loosening the noose a little. "What? What was that?"

"You'll never get away with this," John murmured, barely able to whisper.

"Shiddd let's see," DA welcomed, with a warm laugh. "I got a funny suspicion they'll label the cause of your death as suicide."

DA started pulling the rope continuously until John had no alternative but climb on top of the chair. John was standing on the tips of his toes when DA strung the rope over the banister for a second and third time and tied a knot into it.

"There that should do it," DA grunted, as if his struggles were over. "Any last words Officer John?"

Officer John's eyes bulged as his lips mimicked the words *fuck you.*

"Well if that's how you feel about it," DA ridiculed, kicking the chair from under John. "Then that's how you feel about it."

John's swinging body was having convulsions as his toil came to a quick end.

DA repacked his bag, turned the television off and headed for the door. He took one last look at John's corpse while he opened the door.

"At least they'll be able to get a urine sample from you." DA finished, walking away from the dark open house.

Chapter 3

Vexed

DA found himself awaking to the smell of food. *Sharon must be down there hooking it up,* he thought to himself as his eyes adjusted to the morning light.

"Ahhh," DA yawned, stretching his arms far east and west as he could while he sat up.

DA climbed out of bed, he figured that he would take a shower while Sharon (his latest girlfriend) finished cooking breakfast. He came out of the shower draped in basketball shorts and a robe. He walked downstairs to the kitchen.

A plate of steaming scrambled eggs, hash browns, sausage and French toast sat atop the counter. No one was in the kitchen as DA grabbed the plate from the counter and walked towards the living room.

DA's younger sister Dana sat in the living room. She was focused intently on the morning news while she ate her breakfast. From the looks of the scene on television, something big was going down.

"God's morning baby girl," DA called out, making his presence known.

"God's morning big bruh," Dana spoke, acknowledging her brothers presence with a lingering stare. "Somebody got pissed off this morning and killed a cop. Shit all over the news."

"Yeah," DA said, nonchalantly.

"Yeah. They found his ass hanging," Dana shot back, with her stare ever increasing on her brother.

"They catch who did it?" DA asked, taking a seat next to Dana, and quickly stuffing his mouth with breakfast.

"Naw. So far they're saying it's a possible suicide but I ain't buying that shit," Dana replied. "And check this shit out. I've seen that pig before, I just can't remember where."

Dana sat quietly for a spell watching the latest details as they developed. DA sat quietly knowing his baby sister's suspicions, had been aroused.

"You ain't heard nothing about this until just now?" Dana questioned, with skepticism and without breaking her stare at the television.

"Shit first I'm hearing of it," DA replied, eye's locked on the television.

"You a got damn lie!" Dana burst out shouting. "DA! You gon' sit yo' black ass right here in my face and insult my intelligence."

"Whadda' fuck you howling about," DA questioned, playing the role of Mr. Innocent.

"You know where I know that cop from DA?" Dana asked, quickly regaining her calm. "I know him from a file you kept in your office bruh. That was one of the cops that killed our uncle. Now tell me I'm wrong."

"You wrong," DA answered, eye's locked on the television.

"Ooh, I swear sometimes you niggas ain't shit," Dana yelled, jumping to her feet and pounding one fist into the palm of her other hand. "You not even a good fuckin' liar to make it worst!"

"Baby Girl I'm trying to watch the news and eat breakfast here if you don't mind," DA calmly retorted, giving his baby sister the eye she had grown up learning not to test.

"Nigga I give a fuck about yo' look. That shit don't work no more. You don't scare me," Dana shot back, composing herself and having a seat on the couch again. "Fuck around and get handled, you don't start coughing up some information relevant to what I wanna hear."

DA choked quickly turning his head staring at his sister with a puzzled look and a hard laugh.

"I don't know who yo' little **wanna-be-man** ass think you are," DA returned, with a pointed finger. "But I will knock you the fuck out girl. You got me fucked up…SIR."

"Sir dis' clit nigga," Dana spoke, rising from the couch again and heading for DA's office. "I know what I'm gon' do, imma find that fuckin' file."

DA sprung up from the couch in hot pursuit of Dana at the mentioning of the file. She attempted to slam his office door but DA was too fast and burst through the door before it could close.

"I'm not playing witchu' girl," DA warned. "Don't start going through my shit."

"Nigga I been going through yo' nasty ass shit all my life," Dana replied, leading the chase around her brother's desk. "And ain't shit changing today handsome."

DA was tiring of the *ring around the rosy* game when the doorbell sounded off.

"Yeah go get the door bruh," Dana said, smiling from ear to ear.

"I ain't worried about it," DA replied, shrugging the loss off. "It ain't shit in here anyways! Put my office back the way you found it or I'm throwing your disrespectful ass outta here."

DA strolled out of the room closing the door behind him. It was all a psychological ploy to convince Dana that the file wasn't in the office and he had nothing to worry about. Truth was if she looked hard enough she would find it.

"Who is it?" DA shouted, at the second ringing of his doorbell.

"Open this muthafucka up and see," A voice from the other side screamed back.

DA knew the voice belonged to his longtime friend Crafty.

DA met Crafty when he and Dana were forced to live with their Aunt Betty in South Los Angeles after the murder of their uncle. The two had been closest road dawgs ever since.

"That little sister of yours crazy as a muthafucka man," Crafty announced, walking through the door and giving DA a pound from his fist.

"She about to get her crazy ass whooped right now she don't knock it off with that bullshit," DA replied.

"Oh the little monster here already huh," Crafty said, with a sly smile on his face.

"Yeah and in full bullshit mode," DA answered, closing the door.

"Damn shit smell good in here. What's for breakfast?" Crafty asked.

"Too late soup," DA answered, strolling back to the living room.

"It's a damn shame the way you treat family" Crafty murmured, shaking his head as he followed DA. "Hey but yo' sister. My nigg she pulled a pistol on some dude yesterday, slapped 'em all in his mouth like a little ole hooker."

"No shit," DA questioned, shaking his head and sighing. "Wanna be too hard."

"Yeah her name getting out there bruh," Crafty advised.

"Shit ain't good," DA spoke.

"It never is," Crafty agreed.

"I know you heard about that cop that killed himself this morning," Crafty said. "Shit the way police acting you woulda' thought somebody killed that muthafucka."

"Don't remind me," DA uttered, taking a seat on the living room couch. "Dana screaming about this shit right now."

DA took a seat back on the living room couch and Crafty headed for the living room bar.

"Yo' boy a full blown alcoholic," Dana announced, entering the living room. "Look at 'em, drinking early in the morning."

"Whatever dude!" Crafty retorted.

"You can keep the lesbian jokes to yourself fat boy. Y'all know I'm strictly dickly," Dana spoke, sitting down next to DA. "Why you bullshitting."

"Find what you were looking for?" DA asked, staring his sister down.

"It's ok. I know you have it," Dana answered. "Keep on treating yo' baby sister like one of those punk ass bitches. You gon' need me before I need you."

DA ignored his sister's comments, staying focused on the news broadcast as he continued to eat.

"You know DA's the one who killed that cop Crafty," Dana blurted out.

"WHAT?" Crafty yelled.

"Ok it's time for you to go sis," DA announced, grabbing Dana by the arm. "She full a shit my nigg, don't listen to her."

Dana began to struggle with DA who tried pulling her up from the couch.

"Lemme go," Dana screamed at the top of her lungs. "I ain't going no fucking place."

"Oh yo' little ass leaving here," DA demanded. "I dun' had it up to here with your got damn mouth girl."

Dana struggled, kicking wildly trying to avoid being gaffled. Dana's resistance was so fierce DA backed off for fear of catching a hard knee to his private parts.

"Start that shit again. I swear imma drag yo' ass outta here," DA warned.

"I'm just saying," Dana returned.

"Say it again if you think I'm lying," DA shot back.

"What the fuck is she talking about my nigg," Crafty questioned.

"Nothing. She think the cop that hung himself is the one that killed our uncle," DA pronounced, ever so nonchalantly.

"Is it?" Crafty asked emphatically.

"Shit I don't know," DA answered, focusing back on the news program.

"Hold da' fuck up! You don't know," Crafty yelled, slamming his glass on the bar counter, moving around to the front of the couch and staring straight in DA's face. "Aww my nigg you lying. The fuck you mean you don't know as much as you researched that shit."

"I knew this nigga was lying," Dana yelled abruptly. "Wow my own flesh and bone. My own blood brother finally lied to me on some shit like this. Even dumb ass Crafty know that was some bullshit!"

"Nobody lied to you Dana. You know our get down baby girl," DA argued. "You all I got and we don't lie to each other."

"Well nigga you lied to me," Crafty interjected. "Lying ass muthafucka. How you not gon' tell yo' road dawg. I see why you ain't tell her, she a girl."

"Fuck you! Fat black ass," Dana screamed. "This fat ass nigga can't even run looking like overstuffed ass Flava Flav."

"Nigga you need a man's help to pull this kinda shit off," Crafty yelled, waving Dana's comment off. "Whadda' fuck got you thinking you Bruce Willis around this muthafucka I don't know, but die hard niggas die easy."

"What if something would have happen to you? I wouldn't have known shit DA," Dana bellowed, with the beginning signs of tears starting to well in her eyes.

Both Crafty and Dana were starting to verbally pound DA in a nonstop attack. DA found himself trying to explain to one while the other screamed and vice versa.

DA took a step back screaming "Shut da' fuck up. I don't know shit, I don't know shit. Gotdamn!"

Dana and Crafty went silent, both studying DA's every expression, his every gesture. The room was quiet for all of ten seconds.

"I guess you gon be dragging two muthafuckas outta here this morning," Crafty started. "Cuz that's some bullshit you trying to spoon feed us partner."

"Alright that's enough of both you niggas," DA spoke, pointing his finger at both of them. "Both of y'all get the fuck out."

"Wrong bruh. Nigga ain't going nowhere and now shit on the precipice of explosion," Crafty said.

"Precipice of explosion?" DA and Dana murmured simultaneously.

Crickets could be heard. DA and Dana both stared silently at Crafty with their mouths open.

"This niggas an intelligent retard dude I swear," Dana burst out laughing.

"What the fuck I tell you about using big words Crafty," DA spoke.

"That's my word of the day nigga, WHAT!" Crafty barked. "PRECIPICE NIGGA, means I'm on the verge NIGGA, on the brink NIGGA of tearing some shit the FUCK UP you don't start dosing me with some truth up in this bitch...NIGGA!"

"I'm not gon' be too many more of yo' niggas," DA warned, staring Crafty down.

"That's cool bruh cuz I ain't gon' be too many more of your fools either," Crafty retorted, returning DA's serious stare. "You either give us the truth or we finna have our first rumble homeboy."

"Rat pack session going down in this joint," Dana interrupted, becoming jumpy while cracking her knuckles.

"Nigga I wish a muthafucka would," DA warned, sliding the coffee table back to make extra room. "Space and opportunity nigettes, who first?"

The attack was instant and without words, Crafty charged like a bull seeing red. Crafty tackled DA to the couch with a linebacker's hit that slid the couch two feet. Dana jumped on top of the stack. The couch screeched across the wooden floors as the three wrestled furiously.

"Gaffle his legs, Gaffle his legs," Crafty yelled, trying to hold DA in a pinned position.

The weight of both Dana and Crafty made it difficult for DA to move. He was stuck and feeling smothered.

"Let us in, we'll let you go," Dana urged. "We already know what time it is."

"Alright y'all got me," DA spoke, partially winded from struggle but still offering sporadic challenges.

"This nigga lying again," Crafty interrupted, applying more weight and force. "Put that on something?"

"Yeah put that on something," Dana agreed.

"I put that on everything…if y'all not off of me in the next five seconds I'm popping as soon as I get to my pistol," DA issued. "Now, I put that on something."

"Alright let this nigga go," Crafty stated, rising up from his pinning position. DA was known for giving a flesh wound. "That's how you playing yo' people huh."

"Yeah it's cool," Dana spoke, backing away. "They say all family ain't family."

"OK that just got you thrown out dammit," DA shrieked, rising from the couch. DA was soft for his baby sister and she knew how to push his buttons by questioning his loyalty to her. "Y'all not finna pressure me in my own house."

DA took Dana by the arm and began walking her to the front door.

"Yeah throw her ass out," Crafty said snickering. "This is a penis only club."

"Go to hell fat boy," Dana antagonized. "Yo' tiny dick ass in the wrong club. They said penis not penny."

Dana began to struggle a little as her and DA neared the front door. DA took a firm hold of her.

"Ok big bruh I'm sorry. Please don't throw me out," Dana begged.

DA paused a second while opening the door. He took a brief look at Dana and knew his baby sister wouldn't behave.

"Sorry baby girl," DA said, pushing Dana onto the other side of the door. "Not in the mood."

DA slammed the door closed to the screams of Dana who was going into her Denzel Washington portrayal of Training Day. Crafty walked over joining DA at the door.

"DA! You think you can do this shit to me," Dana mimicked, pointing her fingers at her own chest. "Aww...ok, I'm putting cases on both you bitches," She continued, pointing at Crafty and DA as they stared out the window.

DA and Crafty stared out the window unconcerned, watching Dana as she caused her usual early morning disturbance.

"You muthafuckas will be playing basketball in Pelican's Bay when I'm through with you," Dana continued, with the theatrics. "SHU program nigga, twenty three hour lock down. Who da' fuck? DA! Open the door, DA!"

DA let the curtain fall back into place as he and Crafty walked back to the living room couch. DA dragged the coffee table back in place and began flickering through the channels when his cell phone rang. He checked his caller ID, it was Dana.

"What's up baby girl? I ain't got time for the bullshit." DA spoke, turning the speaker button on and placing the phone next to him on the couch.

"Retired Police Detective John Smith, born November 11th, 1956," Dana started.

DA jumped up and rushed into his office. He pulled an encyclopedia from his bookshelf and opened it. The file was gone. DA was pissed as he marched back into the living room grabbing his phone from the couch and heading to the front door.

"Give me my shit Dana! Stop playing," DA argued, snatching the front door open.

Dana sat in her XJ8 Black Jaguar with the engine running. If DA showed any attempt to approach her car, she'd be in the wind and he knew it.

"I want in big bruh. No ifs, ands or maybes," Dana said softly.

"Hmmm," DA sighed, giving in. "Bring the file back in and let's talk."

"I'll be right in," Dana spurted out, recognizing her brother's defeat.

DA left the door open, strolling back to the couch again. He sat there shaking his head. Crafty could tell his friend was thinking and headed back to the bar to pour another drink. The door slammed shut and Dana was all smiles as she took a seat next to DA. DA sat with a stern face in silence, staring forward.

"I love you big brother," Dana said, grabbing DA's face and placing a big kiss on his cheek.

"Ughh girl. Get off me," DA growled, pulling his face away. "Feel like a man kissing my face."

"Whatever," Dana returned. "So what's the plan DA?"

"Here bruh it looks like you need this," Crafty said, chuckling and passing DA a Hennessey straight with no chaser.

DA took a big gulp of the liquor, placed the glass on the table and looked at both of them. He placed his face in the palms of his hands and took a deep breath.

"Ok...that is the officer that killed our uncle," DA confirmed. "But I didn't kill him. Shit maybe the coward knew I was coming, I don't know but I do know..."

DA's confession was abruptly interrupted by Crafty sliding the coffee table away from the couch with his foot. It stuttered across the floor. DA and Dana looked at the coffee table then pierced upward to notice Crafty's expression. He was stone-faced serious. DA knew he wasn't buying his story.

"Y'all have to do exactly what I tell y'all to do when I tell you to do it," DA commanded. "If you have a problem with that, get the fuck out and I mean that. Understood?"

Dana and Crafty agreed by simple head nods. DA began filling them in on the next mission and their roles.

Chapter 4

Son Of A Bitch

Dana sat in the restaurant sucking on a Vanilla shake as she eyed the establishment. The restaurant was quiet. A small group of customers were finishing their food as Dana waited on Crafty's return from the restroom. Dana scanned the faces of the customers, there was one other black man in the establishment.

Dana shook her head as she watched the black man interact with his five white friends. *Nigga act and sound just like the white boys,* Dana thought to herself.

Crafty returned from the restroom walking down the aisle. Crafty intentionally bumped the black man sitting at the table full of white men.

"Heyyyy," the black man cried out, spilling his drink.

"Excuse me…house nigga," Crafty apologized, staring coldly in the eyes of the black man as he strolled by.

Crafty sat down at the table with Dana. They both laughed at the stunt Crafty had just initiated with the *sellout* black man.

"You almost knock that fool out of his seat," Dana said, laughing in between slurps of her shake.

"Fuck that house nigga," Crafty uttered. "I should have knocked his ass out. Look at him, nigga even dressing like a lil' ole white boy."

Dana and Crafty were certain the group of men were whispering about them. Neither of them gave any concern as they taunted the men with grimacing looks, stares and comments.

"They're only your friend until one of 'em gets mad at you," Dana fired off.

"Which one of 'em fucking you," Crafty spoke, attempting to intimidate the sellout. "Tight pants wearing ass biaaatch."

Crafty mean mugged the entire table of men, briefly stopping to check his watch, it read five minutes until eight o'clock closing time. Crafty took his time eating as if he was observing fine dining etiquette.

Dana's cell phone began to vibrate on the table.

"Yeah," Dana answered, speaking into the phone while watching the group of insulted men file out the door behind one another.

"Say bye you little punk ass bitches!" Crafty hollered, at the men before the door could close all the way.

Dana didn't say a word on the phone, she listened and disconnected the call.

Dana and Crafty eyed one another quickly as the Mexican waiter appeared from the back approaching them.

"Excuse me Sir the restaurant will be closing in two minutes," the waiter informed.

Crafty nodded his head and the waiter was gone.

A young white man who looked like the possible owner appeared from the back with two bags of trash and headed out the back door.

Dana got up from the table and walked towards the rest rooms. The young white man hurried back in nearly bumping Dana.

"Excuse me," The young man said, hurrying back to the kitchen area.

"No problem," Dana returned, opening the door to the ladies room and entering.

The young man reappeared with another two bags and headed towards the back door again. As he passed the ladies room Dana came out in stride following the young man outside.

Crafty got up from the table in pursuit of Dana. He exited the back door to find DA waiting inside a van with the side door open. Dana stood with her gun pointed at the pleading young man, now lying on the ground with a laceration across his left eye.

Dana was giving orders to the man when Crafty walked over, grabbed the young man and dragged him to the van. Dana grabbed the man's legs and her and Crafty tossed the man into the van. Dana and Crafty climbed in the van, closed the door and DA fled the scene as quietly as he had come.

The young man instantly began begging for his life as DA maneuvered the van through the night traffic of Los Angeles.

"I can pay you guys whatever you want," the young man cried. "My family has money."

No one in the van gave the young man any conversation. The ride was as quiet as the dead. Dana and Crafty sat in the back of the van aiming their pistols at the scared man as the rode along.

"You get it from him yet?" DA asked.

Crafty move closer and began searching the man. The man's eyes were glued to Dana and the pistol;

she was clearly aiming at him. Crafty reached in the man's back pockets and pulled the man's cell phone out.

"Got it," Crafty spoke, sliding back towards the front of the van and extending the phone to DA. "Here."

"I don't know you guys and I've never done anything to you," the man said. "Please let me go. I swear this is a mistake."

"Chris Burke! Shut the fuck up," DA announced, alternating his focus between the road and Chris's phone.

"How do you know my name?" Chris questioned.

Dana moved forward slapping the shit out of Chris with her pistol.

"Ahhh!" Chris groaned, grabbing his sore forehead. "What have I done to you?"

"This the last time you gon' be told to shut the fuck up white boy," Dana warned. "Next time shit getting ugly."

Chris went silent as DA took the entrance to the interstate. Dana and Crafty sat smiling at Chris. Chris stayed paralyzed for nearly the entire, half an hour ride.

"I haven't done anything to you," Chris murmured, pleading again. "Please let me go."

Dana started to move forward again but this time Crafty stopped her approach. Crafty dug in the tool box beneath the passenger's seat retrieving a roll of duct tape. He moved closer to Chris tearing a strip of the tape off. Chris nervously huddled against the opposite side of the van.

Crafty attempted to place the tape across the mouth of Chris but Chris had plans of his own. Chris hurled himself forward throwing a soft right hook that didn't budge Crafty's face. Dana's laugh came abruptly causing DA to spy the commotion through his rear view mirror.

Crafty's face frowned up and his hands began to stretch forward.

Chris delivered a quick kick to Crafty's chest that sent Crafty sprawling back across the van. Chris scrambled towards the rear van doors projecting himself like a rocket to burst out and free himself from his captors.

Dana watched the fast exchange incredulously, hunching her shoulder tightly as she watched Chris slam into the rear doors and bounce back falling to the floor in front her unconscious. Chris had knocked himself out.

"Wow two dumb asses," Dana mentioned, under the breath of laughter. "Dumb ass number one can you properly restrain dumb ass number two?"

"Whatever She-Man," Crafty retorted, duct taping the hands, feet and mouth of Chris. "Fool got lucky with that bitch hit."

"Next time, tape his hands first," DA interjected, with a hefty laugh of his own.

"Everybody got jokes today huh," Crafty said, disproving of the comedic session in progress.

The trio rode along for the next hour engaged in their own individual thoughts.

DA pulled off the road near Barstow, California and took a dirt trail that led to an abandoned gas station about two miles from the main road. DA slammed on the brakes and turned off the engine.

The trio exited the van. Crafty snatched Chris by his legs dragging him out of the van; Chris was wide awake now. Chris wiggled his body to free himself from Crafty's grip to no avail. Chris wouldn't calm down until he saw DA approach with a big hunting knife. Chris's eyes widened while his body collapsed in Crafty's arms.

DA squatted in front of Chris cutting the tape that binded his legs together. Chris was stunned. He was expecting to be killed at any moment. Crafty turned Chris's body and DA freed his hands. Chris stood silently shocked as he looked at the three unfriendly faces.

DA snatched the tape covering Chris's mouth and Crafty handed him back his phone.

"Call your father," DA demanded.

Chris studied the faces of the trio trying to understand their actions. His fingers began scrolling quickly through his call list. The phone rang and everyone waited.

"Hello dad," Chris spoke.

Chris's words were immediately cut short and his sudden stutter of interjections apparent. The trio couldn't make out most of the father's screamings but they could hear the curse words flowing.

"Dad!" Chris yelled. "You fucking moron, I've been kidnapped."

The trio could hear the screaming on the other end of the phone stop. DA grabbed the phone from Chris.

"Retired officer Daniel Earl Burke," DA uttered, into the phone.

"Who is this?" Daniel asked. "And what do you want from me?"

"Nothing," DA answered, watching Dana fire one shot through the head of the unexpecting Chris; killing him instantly.

Daniel's body jumped at the sound of the firing pistol.

"Just wanted you to hear the death of your son," DA finished.

The single shot being heard through the phone, shattered the world of Daniel Burke with the force of a ten point earthquake. His body and soul jumped when he heard the distinct sound of gunfire. Christopher was his only child.

DA could hear the moans of the retired officer as he screamed his son's name over and over through the phone. DA dropped the phone on the body of Chris, the trio climbed back in the van and were headed back to LA.

"I know that muthafuckas head right now is fucked up," Dana spoke, breaking the silence.

"Yeah right now he trying to figure out what's going on," Crafty added.

"Well, he better hurry up cause he's on borrowed time," DA chimed in, glaring at Dana through the rear view. "You ok baby girl?"

"I think I'm gon' throw up," Dana replied, curling herself into the fetal position, wrapping herself with her arms tightly. "Bruh! Bruh!"

"What's up Dana?" DA inquired, concerned about his sister's presence of mind. "What you need?"

"Ahhh," Dana groaned, seemingly ailing in pain.

"What's wrong Dana?" DA questioned again, growing more concerned.

"I need…I need…I need a blunt," Dana said, rising slowly from the van floor with the brightest smile and the loudest laughter.

DA and Crafty stared at the pretending Dana.

"What nigga! Shit I need to get high after I put in work," Dana spouted.

"She on that bullshit again homie," Crafty interrupted, shaking his head.

"If you gon' start that bullshit Dana lemme know so I can make other arrangements," DA stated.

"Y'all the ones on that bullshit," Dana fired back. "Thinking yo' baby sister so soft I can't handle myself. Y'all got me fucked up. My murder game official nigga."

"Aww you taking it the wrong way Dana," DA urged.

"Shut up and drive before I shoot you," Dana threatened.

"Moving on," DA shot back. "Make sure y'all keep a low profile and get ready, phase two is less than five days away people."

Chapter 5

Custom Built, Special Delivery

Daniel Burke spent the time preparing his mind for his only son's funeral in the morning. The near past week had been one of the toughest weeks of his life to endure and remain sane. The killer of his child had not been apprehended or identified and his ex-wife blamed him for the death of their son.

Daniel's ex-wife cursed his very existence as she tried to slap skin from his cheeks. Her last words to him were still ringing in his ear, *hell has a special place for evil men like you.*

Daniel sat down on the edge of his bed as his tears started free falling from his eyes. He tried his hardest to control his fluttering emotions but the loss left him just borderline of falling to pieces, someone had murdered his son.

It was 7:30 pm as Daniel wiped his eyes and read the clock on his wall. He was frustrated from not being allowed to participate in the search for his son's killer. No longer being a cop, he wasn't privy to classified information but he still had his resources within the department.

Daniel reached for his cell phone, he was calling in a long awaited debt. Daniel scrolled through his contacts and tapped his screen. A voice on the other end of the call answered.

"I need to see you ASAP," Daniel stated, grabbing a 357 revolver from beneath his pillow, checking it and placing back under the pillow.

The voice on the other end quickly tried to inform Daniel that he couldn't be seen with him and that he was risking his job merely talking to Daniel now.

"Look here you son of a bitch," Daniel interjected. "You owe me one!"

The voice on the other end found no sympathy as Daniel disconnected the call, grabbed his jacket and headed out the door mumbling obscenities.

Daniel had spent the last few days investigating his son's death on his own. He researched his own past to see if any old enemies had been newly freed. He was looking at anyone with the capacity to kill an officer but came up short time and time again.

Daniel sped through traffic throwing caution to the wind as his vehicle weaved in and out of the lanes like a race car. He had taken this route for the past 25 years; this had to be a record time.

Daniel pulled in front of Newton Police Station illegally parking. He jumped out and headed in the building.

Numerous officers gave their condolences and promised their individual support as Daniel made his way to the room housing the homicide detectives.

Daniel was legendary in the cop world. He was as crooked as they come and as evil as one could get. He felt good receiving praise and honor from his former colleagues while he strolled the hallways. The walk through the building was nostalgic for Daniel. It had been a long time. The good memories began replaying in his mind until he reached the homicide squad room door, then his anger re-emerged.

Daniel burst through the homicide detective's door causing all heads to turn in his direction as he made a bee line through the desks. Homicide detective Jack Barnes spied Daniel through his office window and was the first to approach him.

"Dan what the hell are you doing here?" Jack questioned, angrily storming out of his office in Daniel's direction. "You trying to blow this case for us. That's all we need is you lingering around the very detective's working your son's case. You're giving the lawyer ammunition to dismiss this case and set this bastard free. You know how this works Dan."

Jack was right, Daniel knew exactly how the system worked. Daniel wasn't willing to see this killer set free on some bullshit technicality. He was determined to see own brand of justice served.

"I want answers Jack and I want 'em now," Daniel returned.

"Let me work this case Dan," Jack pleaded, hugging his shoulders and escorting Daniel back towards his office. "You know we all want this asshole just as bad as you do but you have to let us do our job."

"I'm going crazy waiting outside the loop Jack," Daniel said, taking a seat at Jack's desk. "Allow me to be an unofficial consultant on this case. You know I'll catch this fucker."

"Can't do it Dan. Too much media coverage," Jack responded. "Any incident with you and this case is shot to hell. Let us find this guy first."

"Jack you owe me one," Daniel said, pointing his finger across the desk at Jack. "This asshole isn't going to prison, he's going in a box. You understand me Jack?"

"Hey! Don't dick around on this one," Jack warned. "You still have enemies who don't care about your current situation and they'll bury you the first time you fart loudly. You think they give a shit about you or your son?"

"Fuck them!" Daniel yelled. "My son is DEAD Jack and theirs is going to college. You think I give a shit about them! To hell with 'em all Jack. How would you feel if it was your son Jack, tell me...tell me Jack!"

Jack stood up, walking over to the door and closing it and the window blinds.

"Listen Dan, as soon as we find this asshole I'll give you all the time I can to deal with him personally before I issue a warrant out for him," Jack confided, taking a seat behind his desk. "But you have to let us find him first Dan. Ok?"

Daniel understood the truth as he heard it. Jack was a stand up cop from the old school and Daniel trusted his word.

"Ok Jack," Daniel replied, raising up from his chair, walking to the door and opening it. "I'll be waiting on your call."

Daniel closed the door and headed out of the building. He stood for a brief moment sucking in the fresh air. He started walking to his car when a voice called out him.

"Hey Dan," Jack yelled, catching up to him. "How about a drink? I'm buying."

"Sure why not," Daniel answered. "I got nothing but time."

Daniel followed Jack to their old after hour hangout.

Daniel and Jack sat at the table throwing back shots of Tequila.

"Forensics came up clean, the neighbors haven't heard or seen anything suspicious, this guy has been lucky so far," Jack whispered, swallowing his glass. "But he's bound to slip up."

"They always do," Daniel agreed, gulping down his own glass. "When he does, I'll have his pine box waiting...custom built and special delivery."

The two men sat around for another 20 minutes discussing Daniel's mindset. Daniel was convinced that there was something the detectives were overlooking or simply had missed.

"There's gotta be something," Daniel continued, pondering over every word of the brief exchange he shared with his son's killer. "He said he wanted nothing except for me to hear my son being murdered. It's gotta be a personal grudge."

"We've gone through your complete history with a microscope," Jack replied. "There's no old collars looking for payback here."

"This isn't random," Daniel said. "I just can't get my head around it at the moment."

"Don't worry too much," Jack uttered. "We got our best guys on it. They'll find this asshole and you'll have your moment alone with him. You can count on that."

The two men clinked their glasses together, gulped down the last of the alcohol and headed out the bar.

Chapter 6

Together Forever

DA, Dana and Crafty sat in the truck watching their target.

"What the fuck is he doing now?" Dana spoke, seemingly agitated. "I knew we should have grabbed his ass earlier."

DA glanced over at Dana in the driver's seat. He had already made his warning clear. His eye pierce was solely a reminder to Dana that it was his way or the highway.

Everyone sat in the truck silently watching as the two men hugged and parted ways.

"Detective Jack Barnes," DA whispered, silently to himself.

"What?" Crafty asked, leaning forward in his seat.

"Nothing," DA answered. "Just talking to myself homie."

DA fell into deep thought staring out the window as he temporarily pondered.

"Alright let's go," DA ordered.

Dana guided the truck through the city streets.

"You and Crafty check out that shit I asked y'all," DA questioned.

"Yeah it was just the way you figured," Dana replied. "The place closes at eight but we found an entry point on the other side."

"Cool then it's on and crackin' tonight," DA responded.

"Yeah buddy," Crafty echoed out, excited about the impending mission. "It's time to get this muthafucka."

"Everyone who participated getting the death sentence," Dana stated adamantly.

"Yeah let's go get ready," DA said. "We got about an hour before he gets back."

Dana maneuvered through traffic; racing the truck up the freeway on ramp.

"Slow down girl, Gotdamn," Crafty urged. "We on schedule."

"Yeah. What the fuck you rushing for?" DA inquired.

"I'm sorry y'all," Dana apologized. "I'm a little anxious bruh. I been waiting fa' payback a long time now."

DA looked at Dana while Crafty stared at her through the rear-view mirror. Both men could see the tears lightly flooding her eyes. DA knew her sentiments well and returned an empathetic glance. Crafty reached over the seat rubbing Dana on her shoulder.

"It's ok baby girl," Crafty spoke, softly attempting to ease her pain. "You getting payback tonight and that's a promise."

Dana slowed her speed and began cruising. They were on their way to Sun Valley. It was time for a direct visit.

Dana pulled over and turned off the engine. The crew put on gloves and Crafty draped his shoulders with a back pack.

"Y'all ready to get busy," DA asked, eyeing the pair.

The answer was a unanimous yes as the crew prepared to step out of the vehicle.

"Hey," DA shot out, grabbing Dana by the arm. "Stick to the plan, nothing fancy and above all Dana…be careful."

"I'm cool bruh and besides I got you watching my back," Dana replied, giving her bright smile a full display. "I couldn't buy more loyal protection."

"I know that's right," Crafty joined in.

DA smiled and the crew stepped out of the vehicle.

Dana parked the suburban two blocks over. The street was a dead end. It had a brick wall that separated the houses from a water canal used to direct water away from the homes along the hills.

DA and Dana climbed the small brick and waited as Crafty struggled to get over.

The crew moved along the wall in the dark of the night. Daniel lived in the last house nearest the brick wall one block further. The crew was looking for the X marking on the wall. DA had placed the X on the wall a few days previous, it was to let himself know exactly where Daniel's backyard started.

"Here it go," DA whispered, referring to the X marking.

The wall separating Daniel's property from the canal at this point was five and a half feet tall.

"You need some help with this one?" DA questioned, looking at Crafty.

"Naw I got it," Crafty answered, jumping up on the wall and pulling himself over first.

DA and Dana followed suit, quickly scurrying over the wall.

"Keep your heat off safety," DA warned. "Anything looks funny, we dump it out and push."

"I'm liking these silencers you came up on DA," Crafty said, giving his pistol a final inspection. "Nigga feeling like 007 around this bitch."

DA and Dana offered a slight smile following Crafty towards the back door.

"Is that right? Well watch the corner of the house and try not to get us busted 007," DA joked, while Dana attempted to pick the door lock.

"Got it," Dana whispered, turning the knob and entering the house.

DA gestured for Crafty to follow as he entered the house. Crafty followed, closing the door behind him and drew the shades close.

Crafty took off the back pack and pulled out flashlights passing them to Dana and DA.

"Y'all know what to do," DA spoke, as the crew went their separate ways throughout the house searching.

DA had been to the address before but had never entered the house. He glanced in room after room on the lower level of the house. He stopped at what seemed to be an office of sorts. DA entered the room looking for anything that would help solve some of his questions.

DA search the room for nearly five minutes before Dana showed up carrying three pistols.

"DA you was right again bruh," Dana said. "This old fool strapped for real. I found these three in the bedroom alone."

"Take the shells out and put the guns back exactly like you found them." DA ordered.

DA had already taken the shells out of a shot gun and a pistol stashed in the office. DA searched the other rooms emptying any guns found and placing them back in order.

Dana rushed back downstairs running into DA at the bottom of the staircase.

"Where Crafty?" DA asked Dana.

"I thought he was with you," Dana responded.

The two moved out in search of Crafty.

"I betchu' that big ole nigga in the kitchen," Dana speculated, as they moved about. "Find the kitchen, we find Crafty."

Crafty sat at the kitchen table enjoying himself a sandwich when DA and Dana walked in. Crafty had four pistols stretched across the table that he had found.

"At least you did some work first," Dana said.

"Y'all can look at me any way y'all want. I don't give a fuck," Crafty said, studying the faces of the disapproving DA and Dana. "Work make me hungry."

"Dude should be pulling up shortly so let's get ready," DA warned. "Crafty take the shells out of the guns, put 'em back where you found them and get rid of the fucking sandwich. Be careful, it's a good chance dude might be carrying a gun on him."

Crafty emptied the guns placing them back where they belonged once he finished his sandwich. He hid in the pantry when he heard the motorized garage door opening. It was time for justice.

Daniel staggered in the house and closed the door. He took his jacket off and went to the kitchen. Daniel reached up in the cabinet retrieving a bottle of scotch and a glass. He was already drunk but trying to drink himself into a coma. Daniel slammed the glass on the counter, opening the bottle and drinking straight from it. Daniel left the glass on the counter and took the bottle upstairs with him to the bedroom.

Daniel kicked his shoes off while holding the bottle upside down. The bottle was completely empty when Daniel fell back on his pillow slapping himself in the head with it. Daniel rolled over thankfully blacking out. His son's funeral was in the morning and thinking about it was something he rather not do.

Daniel laid still as the room spent around him. He felt like he had slept for hours and still he felt drunk. He tried closing his eyes for a second to get his head under control. Daniel was starting to feel a little better with a hangover. He continued to lay lifeless against his pillow. He had been hearing voices while he slept but wasn't sure he was dreaming.

Daniel's eyes opened again slightly more this time. A silhouette out of the corner of his eye caught his attention. Daniel knew someone was standing in his bedroom. He folded his arms under his pillow and adjusted his position while pretending to still be in deep sleep.

Daniel became nervous when he noticed a second silhouette standing next to the first one at the foot of his bed. Daniel began wiggling as if he was tossing and turning, his name was being whispered again.

Daniel rolled over abruptly sitting partially up and clicking his gun repeatedly.

Crafty turned the bedroom lights on, DA tossed Daniel the shells to his revolver and Dana focused her pistol directly at Daniel's head.

Daniel studied the faces of the group unphazed. "You're the bastards that killed my son aren't you? Who the fuck are you?"

"Does the name Darryl Arrington ring a bell with you?"

Daniel gave a slight grin as he stared DA eye to eye.

"So that's what this is all about huh," Daniel said, falling into a long laugh. "You killed John didn't you?"

"Yes I did," DA proudly acknowledged, moving closer to the side of the bed.

"I'm not scared of you," Daniel announced, spitting in DA direction. "Whoever the hell you are."

"Darryl Arrington Jr," DA pronounced slowly, before punching Daniel clean in the jaw and taking his pistol.

Daniel rolled over in bed still laughing until Dana jumped in the bed straddling him. Dana pistol whipped Daniel for all of thirty seconds until DA and Crafty could manage to pull her off of him. Daniel looked up bleeding from his eyes, nose and mouth but still laughing.

"And whose the angry violent little bitch with you," Daniel asked, smiling while wiping blood from his face.

"Bitch! Who da' fuck you calling bitch cracka?" Dana howled.

"Dana feel free to reintroduce yourself," DA offered, freeing Dana of his grip.

"Gladly bruh," Dana replied, stepping closer to Daniel and slapping him another two times while pronouncing her full name. "Dana Arrington pig and don't forget it."

Crafty stepped over towards the bed and began dragging Daniel off of it. DA joined in to control the struggling Daniel. The two men had Daniel gaffled in no time and proceeded down the stairs with him.

"All right baby girl handle your business," DA instructed. "Watch out and be careful."

"I got this bruh," Dana stated, walking out the back door and disappearing over the wall.

DA sat watching Daniel at gun point while Crafty waited at the garage door for Dana. The garage door began to lift and Crafty turned off the garage light while Dana backed the suburban in. Once the garage door was back down Crafty turned the lights back on.

Dana and Crafty began covering the back of the truck with plastic. This is where Daniel was to be placed as they transported him to the next location. Crafty and Dana made sure to tape the plastic up to the beginning of the window covering the complete inside paneling. There was to be no traces of Daniel in the back of the suburban.

"We ready," Crafty alerted, stepping back in the house.

"On your feet Daniel," DA instructed.

Daniel struggled all the way to the garage. He was taking the first opportunity presented to escape. Those plans were foiled when he noticed Crafty undoing a strip of duct tape. Crafty taped his feet together with his hands behind his back.

Crafty undid one more strip to cover his mouth. No one wanted to hear a grown man begging.

Daniel was tossed in the back of the truck like a sack of potatoes. The crew loaded up and pulled out of Daniel's garage on their way to Hollywood.

It was a little after midnight when Dana pulled to the backside of Forest Lawn cemetery. She turned off the engine and the trio stepped out of the truck. DA and Crafty unloaded the truck of Daniel. Crafty hoisted Daniel over his shoulder and began heading for the entry point as the others followed.

The entry on the backside was a cut through some tall brush and a hole in the gate. Dana widened the hole in the gate by pulling and stretching it. DA and Crafty passed through with no problem even with Daniel over his shoulder.

Crafty led the way across the cemetery to a hole in the ground intended for Daniel's son. Crafty placed Daniel on the ground standing him up. DA cut the tape from his hands, feet and mouth.

Daniel figured he had better take the opportunity now to escape. He figured out the trio's plan to bury him in a grave intended for his son. Daniel struck quickly, hitting Crafty in the jaw and pushing DA to the ground and making a run for it.

Dana broke out after him, DA was up from the ground and in hot pursuit of Daniel also. Dana was the first to catch up to Daniel tackling him to the ground. Daniel rolled over on top of Dana firing right and left fist at her face. Dana was able to avoid the first one but the second fist struck with amazing power dazing her tremendously.

Daniel was on his feet again and moving fast but DA was able to close the gap between them. Daniel could feel DA reaching out for his shoulder. Daniel stopped on a dime causing DA to miss his grip on Daniel and fly pass him. DA attempted to regain his balance stumbling pass Daniel. DA was able to grab the bottom of Daniel's pants leg tripping him up.

DA quickly topped Daniel attempting to strike him with punches. Daniel preferred to wrestle and grabbed a hold of DA tussling with him on the ground instead. Daniel got his hands on DA's gun and tried to point it in DA's direction. One shot fired off missing DA's head by inches as he and Daniel struggled for the gun.

Crafty appeared slapping Daniel in the back of the head with a shovel and knocking him unconscious. DA and Crafty dragged the unconscious Daniel back to the site, tossing his body into the grave. Daniel came to as his body hit the dirt.

"You assholes will never get away with this," Daniel screamed.

"You cops need a new line," Crafty said. "That shit sounds Hollywood."

"John said the same thing," DA added, swinging his head from side to side, glancing at his cohorts. "Still here though. Unfortunately I can't say the same for you."

The trio stood surrounding the grave. Dana pulled her pistol and DA and Crafty followed suit. The trio took aim of Daniel as he laid motionless.

"You don't scare me. I'm not afraid of dying," Daniel uttered, from the grave. "I've been waiting on this moment for a long time."

"Good news then Daniel," Dana interrupted. "Your wait is finally over."

"I'll give you one chance to earn your way out of this grave," DA spoke, urging Daniel to accept. "Tell me who was pulling your strings when you and those devils killed my uncle and you'll be able to climb out of this grave."

"Go to hell nigger," Daniel yelled.

The trio began firing multiple shots. Daniel's body seemed to dance as each shell entered him. The trio watched as Daniel's eyes began closing slowly. Crafty took careful aim and fired one last shot to the head of Daniel. Crafty's bullet found its mark and Daniel was finally dead. Dana grabbed the shovel and hurled a load of dirt in the grave partially covering Daniel's face.

"Ungrateful muthafucka," Dana yelled, looking serious as ever. "He didn't even thank us for joining him and his son together forever."

Chapter 7

Hot Pockets

Dana sat at home watching MTV with her live-in boyfriend. Pockets was a young psychotic with a bad temper, he also possessed an affinity for repetitive speech and discussing himself in the third person.

They were arguing about Dana's whereabouts the night before. Dana didn't get home until late and Pockets was furious.

"Nigga I don't owe you no explanations," Dana stated. "I don't know who da' fuck you think you talking to but you better hurry up and put some respect in your tone."

"Bitch what! You better check yo' mouth when you talking to Pockets. Pockets don't play dat shit," Pockets spoke, referring to himself in the third person. "You already cruising for a bruising round dis' muthafucka. Betta' start talking bout' where yo' ass was at last night."

"If you dream about putting hands on me, Pockets better wake yo' ass up and make you apologize nigga," Dana said, giving Pockets the evil eye. "It don't take much to make a nigga like you disappear."

"The only thing that's gon' disappear round dis' bitch, is gon' be my foot in yo' ass," Pockets threatened. "Let me find out you cheating on me and see if the grim reaper don't show up in this muthafucka. Everybody going bye-bye gotdammit!"

Dana knew the argument was a serious one but she had a quick fix for it. She only continued it to hear Pockets scream in anger. This was the only way she knew Pockets to express any of his love for her.

"Aww! My boo jealous," Dana teased, wrapping her arms around Pockets and kissing his cheek. "That's so cute."

"We'll see how cute shit is when I lay one of these bitch ass niggas down," Pockets spoke, continuing with his threats. "Now where the fuck were you last night and I'm not playing Dana."

"Ok. Ok I was with my brother and Crafty last night," Dana admitted. "Seriously I was helping my brother with some business. I swear."

"Business huh?" Pockets questioned, skeptically. "What the fuck happened to yo' face? Who hit my woman?"

Dana thought about the punch Daniel hit her with last night. Her yellow skin could never hide a bruise. She didn't notice it last night but it was here now. She couldn't tell Pockets the truth and she couldn't give any name. Pockets was a true serial killer and Dana knew anyone she blamed would soon be murdered.

"I got into with some lesbo yesterday over her bitch looking at me," Dana began pouring out her lie. "When I wasn't looking, the bitch hit me with a stick and ran. I was hot but I let that shit go."

Pockets was in a full stare from the moment he heard lesbo come out Dana's mouth. He knew she was being untruthful but not why. Dana disliked lesbians with a passion. It was part of her childhood. With Dana being a tom boy, lesbians were constantly targeting her. Dana had been making examples out of those bitches since her young days.

"So you was witcho' bruh yesterday?" Pockets inquired, just for certainty.

"Yes Pockets. I swear," Dana pledged. "I ain't gon' get nobody killed fucking with yo' psychotic ass. You my little psycho."

"Why you be playing so much," Pockets asked. "That shit ain't cool girl, that shit ain't cool."

"I just like seeing you get jealous," Dana told teasingly. "You be going on one boo. That shit is sexy."

"Sexy to you is pissing me off huh?" Pockets asked rhetorically.

"You'll kill for this pussy huh?" Dana questioned, continuing her tease. "Yeah I see it nigga, you'll kill for this pussy. You better, cause' I'm sho' gon' kill bout my dick. Let me catch you out here flossin' with one of these bitches, they'll be identifying YOU and HER by y'all muthafuckin' dental records."

Pockets glanced at Dana shaking his head while he rolled a blunt. He knew she was crazy and he loved it. A knock on the door diverted both of their attention.

"Who is it?" Pockets called out, sitting the blunt on the table and rising from the couch.

The knocking grew louder and quicker.

"Nigga who the fuck is it?" Pockets yelled, snatching the door open. "Aww it's dis' nigga."

Pockets turned away from the door swinging it closed in the face of DA. Pockets returned to blunt rolling while DA stepped in the house to the welcome of Dana. Dana rose from the couch hugging her brother.

"I see a nigga still on his period in this bitch huh," DA said, staring Pockets down hard as he returned his sister's hug.

"Bruh don't come over here starting shit today," Dana quickly interjected.

"I'm not," DA rebutted, looking as innocent as possible. "But, you did see that little bitch move, he pulled just then right?"

"Bitch move," Pocket screamed. "I got yo' bitch move right here in my boxers nigga, right here in my boxers."

"Dana I thought I told you to find a real man once you got grown," DA antagonized, taking a seat in the recliner next to the couch. "I'm so disappointed in yo' choice."

Pockets tried ignoring DA's comments as he lit the blunt. He stared straight ahead at the television, quickly chanting about himself in the third person again. "Pockets watching videos, Pockets watching videos. Pockets can't hear dis' nigga, Pockets can't hear dis' nigga."

"Baby girl, that's why he's supposed to be taking his medication," DA spoke, offering his opinion.

"Need to put that weed down and pick up that Thorazine."

"I'm not feeling this bullshit that y'all on," Dana interrupted. "Both y'all niggas need to chill on that extra masculinity stuff, that shit ain't cool."

Both men glared in Dana's direction in disbelief.

"Masculinity?" DA said, surprised by Dana's comment.

"DA you can get the fuck out right now," Dana spoke, putting her brother on notice.

"Damn I ain't even said shit," DA protested.

"Nigga yo' lips were moving faster than your words," Disrespect me and I'm throwing yo' ass out. That's all I got to say."

"Nigga lips moving, nigga lips moving," Pockets added, still staring straight ahead at the television while blowing a cloud of smoke in the air.

DA smiled and shook his head at Pocket's comments.

"Baby girl, I'm gon' need yo' help again tonight," DA said, looking around the house.

"She can't go," Pockets blurted out, initiating another argument between himself and DA. "I don't trust you."

"You don't trust me!" DA yelled. "I'm her brother nigga. I don't trust you."

"You slipping DA," Pockets uttered. "My woman got hurt fucking with you. You haven't noticed her face have you?"

Dana closed her eyes, praying that DA wouldn't kill her lie. "Pockets I told you what happen yesterday."

"You think I believed that bullshit you tried feeding me about a lesbian hitting you and you let it go," Pockets said, staring Dana in her face.

DA rose from the chair and took close examination of his sister's face. His facial expression told his anger.

DA knew where the bruise came from and sat back down silently angered. He hadn't noticed the bruise last night.

"Yeah explain that shit DA," Pockets urged. "She ain't going."

"You can't tell me where and when I'm going," Dana argued.

"I just did," Pockets replied.

"The nigga might be right this time," DA uttered, thinking about the bruise on Dana and how it could have been much worse. DA would die before he allowed Dana to get hurt again.

Pockets was stunned by DA's agreement and Dana was now furious.

"I don't give a fuck about what neither one of you niggas talking about," Dana shot back quickly. "I'm going!"

"Then I'm going to," Pockets demanded.

"This family business," DA interrupted. "Ain't got shit to do with you partner."

"She my woman," Pockets rebutted. "Since you can't protect my woman when she with you, I guess I have to."

Dana knew that comment would anger DA, he prided himself on protecting his baby sister.

"Protect your woman?" DA yelled, standing to his feet and moving to the center of the living room. "Nigga protect yo' self."

"Yeah this is what Pockets been waiting for," Pockets said, rising from the couch and joining DA in the middle of the living room. "A man up session."

Dana felt a physical fight was brewing and leapt across the table to intervene.

"Uh unn," Dana yelled, standing in between the two men. "Ain't no fighting in my shit!"

DA hovered over the smaller Dana and Pockets daring him to throw a punch. Pockets danced around Dana looking for a strike point.

"Both of y'all niggas stop it," Dana screamed to the top of her lungs.

"Naw that nigga wants a man up session," DA said, attempting to move around Dana. "I'll man his ass up. Nigga think he's hard cuz he gotta few dumb asses under his wing."

"Naw nigga, you think you hard cuz you can throw a few dollars around," Pockets refuted. "I don't give a fuck about a rich bitch nigga."

"Stop it y'all," Dana screamed, pushing DA back towards the recliner.

"The day my sister fall outta love with you Pockets is the day I'm gon' fall in love with you," DA said. "Imma love kicking yo' ass."

Pockets waved DA off and took a seat back on the couch. Even though Pockets was much smaller than DA, Pockets had no fear of him whatsoever. Pockets was the epitome of a gangster.

The truth was DA respected Pockets. DA knew Pockets loved Dana and on more than one occasion, Pockets proved that he would remove any threat to her. DA was cool with that, he simply wanted Pockets to understand that Dana had a brother fully with the business.

DA scanned the house looking at the family pictures displayed on the wall. DA focused on a picture of his mother and his Aunt Betty. They were two beautiful women and both were deceased. Aunt Betty had taken care of them after the death of their uncle and had passed away five years ago.

DA vaguely remembered anything about his parents, Dana remembered nothing. They were seven and two years old when they're parents were murdered. Until recently they were under the belief that both their parents died in a car accident. It was better that way for the sanity of the young children, the aunt and uncle agreed.

Deceased Officer John Smith however, told of a different scenario. DA still hadn't shared that bit of information with Dana.

DA glanced at the various pictures of family members. Pictures of his mother and father had always made DA feel empty.

DA smiled warmly as he thought about Aunt Betty's consistent love. She was the only bright light of DA and Dana's childhood.

The sunlight peering through the window momentarily lit the picture vaguely exposing a silhouette unnoticed before.

DA strained his eyes focusing on the picture. DA stood up and walked over to the picture mounted on the wall. The silhouette was gone. It was only visible from the angle in which DA was sitting. The picture itself was old and had slightly lighter spots on portions of its outer perimeter.

DA pulled the picture of the wall, flipping it in his hands. This was strange he thought as he handled the frame. The frame was somehow sealed. DA couldn't open it.

"DA what are you doing?" Dana questioned, looking at him strangely.

DA didn't answer, he smashed the picture on the corner of the table and sent Dana into a frenzy.

"Nigga you dun lost yo' muthafucka mind," Dana screamed, jumping up and attacking DA. "You broke my picture of mama and auntie."

"Nigga dun' fucked up, nigga dun' fucked up," Pockets chanted loudly, watching as Dana applied slaps to DA's head, shoulder's and back.

DA ignored the slaps, concentrating on the removing picture from the frame.

"Chill baby girl," DA screamed. "Look!"

Dana stopped swinging long enough to see DA holding a key in his hand. DA, Dana and Pockets all stared at the key in shock.

"That key was in that picture the whole time?" Pockets questioned, in disbelief. "That picture been hanging on that wall since I start fucking with you. Y'all know what it go to?"

Dana had no clue what the key went to and shook her head no.

"I think this is what Aunt Betty called the key to our life," DA spoke softly. "Remember how Aunt Betty would always tell us she held the key to our life."

"Yeah," Dana yelled, instantly remembering. "I always thought it was the juice talking."

"Naw it wasn't the juice talking baby girl," DA responded, flipping the key in his hand.

The three of them stared at the key pondering what it belonged to. The key had a number on it 282.

"I wonder if it go to a safety deposit box," Pockets said.

"I ain't never known Aunt Betty to have a safety deposit box, you DA?" Dana asked, thinking to herself.

"Naw me neither," DA answered, thinking hard as possible. "Hey, all of Aunt Betty's stuff still in the garage?"

"Yeah it is," Dana spoke. "We ain't touch nothing since she passed."

"We have to search through everything she left," DA demanded, walking towards the back door, heading for the garage.

Dana and Pockets followed while DA made a call to Crafty.

"I need yo' help bruh over here at Dana's immediately," DA implored.

"Don't tell me Pockets over there beating dat ass," Crafty joked, laughing aloud on the other end of the phone.

"Yeah and hurry up," DA answered, pushing the end button.

Chapter 8

Coming Home

Crafty pulled up 20 minutes later and spotted the three, elbows deep in boxes. Pockets was the first to notice Crafty walking up the driveway.

"My nigga, my nigga. What it do Crafty?" Pockets greeted, pulling his hands from the boxes and giving Crafty a hug and handshake. "How you doing?"

"I'm good Peoples," Crafty answered, returning Pocket's hug and handshake. "How you doing?"

"I could be betta," Pockets replied, instantly glaring over in DA's direction. "But it is, what it is."

"Crafty we need yo' hands man," DA insisted. "We have to look through every book, box and paper in this garage. We trying to find anything talking about a key, especially with the number 282 on it."

"Fo Sho. I got you," Crafty responded, looking at a stack of boxes next to Dana. "Wassup baby girl?"

"Wassup Crafty," Dana replied. "Here Crafty, you can start with these boxes here."

Crafty joined the search. The group informed Crafty of the picture incident while they continued to tear through box after box. Including the time for breaks and arguments, the group was four and half hours into it before they found something revealing.

It was a small torn piece of paper with a name, phone number and the number 282 on it. The hand written number 282 wasn't a coincidence the group agreed, nor was its hiding location. The note was found in a small book titled "Truth," on page 282.

"How da' fuck brain cell less here find it?" DA questioned.

"Cuz I'm thinker retard," Pockets answered, pulling his cell phone from his belt clip and staring at the piece of paper. "Every book I check, I check page 282. Boo Yah. Now watch this next Sherlock Holmes moment and learn something…you old dummy."

"My baby so smart," Dana said, hugging and kissing Pockets. "You show 'em baby."

"Nigga an idiot," DA fired off quickly. "So what you doing now Sherlock?"

"Got damn nigga! Will you please let Pockets do what Pockets do," Pockets yelled, irritated by another one of DA's comments. "Pockets finna' get the scoop on all this."

"My bad," DA replied, raising both hands shoulder high and leaning backwards.

The group stood around as Pockets awaited an answer to the call he made.

"Hello," Pockets answered, in a hurry as the group huddled closer to hear the exchange. "Yeah I need two large pizzas for delivery."

"Aww that's that bullshit man," DA burst out in criticism. "Told you this nigga was an idiot."

"Nigga you ordering pizza," Crafty added. "When we trying to solve a mystery. Dawg this nigga here."

"I was just fucking around," Pockets joked, laughing at the two men quickly assuming. "The phone still ringing dumb ass. Boy these niggas here, these niggas here."

No one answered the phone so Pockets called again.

"Gimme' the phone man," DA said, snatching the phone from Pocket's hand. "Ain't nobody got time for his bullshit!"

The phone was still ringing when DA placed it to his ear. It rang two more times before someone answered.

"Thank You for calling First Republic. This is Deborah Williams's secretary and how may I help you?" The voice announced softly.

The name on the paper read D. Williams, this had to be her.

"Hi, my name is Darryl Arrington and I'd like to speak with Ms. Williams please," DA spoke, in his business tone.

"In regards to," The secretary asked.

"282. She'll understand," DA responded, hoping that Ms. Williams would remember something about the key.

"Will you please hold while I try to connect you," The secretary asked, before DA's ears were flooded with the kind of music you hear in elevators. The secretary had put DA on hold before he had a chance to reply.

"Sure," DA spoke to the music. "I'm on hold."

"Why you didn't tell 'em Aunt Betty's name," Dana questioned.

"I didn't think of it," DA answered, hunching his shoulders and putting the phone on speaker.

A woman's voice spoke hastily, interrupting the music to announce herself.

"Hi. This is Ms. Williams. Who is this?" The woman asked.

"Hi ma'am, this is Darryl Arrington," DA started, before the woman cut him off.

"What is this, some kind of joke?" Ms. Williams questioned. "I assure you, it's not funny."

"No ma'am, this is no joke I swear," DA answered, in a rush. "I and my sister where going through…"

"Your sister!" Ms. Williams interjected, seemingly very interested about Dana. "What is your sister's name sir?"

The group studied one another's eyes at Ms. Williams's intense mentioning of Dana's name.

"My sister name is Dana," DA pronounced.

The group all stood around amazed as they listened to Ms. Williams recite Dana's name in unison with DA. She already knew who they were.

"How old are you and your sister currently," Ms. Williams inquired.

"I'm 25 and my sister is 20," DA told.

"O' my god! I can't believe this," She muttered, sounding if she had just taken a deep breath. "Darryl, are you or your sister in possession of the key?"

"Yes Ma'am, we are," DA answered.

Ms. Williams ordered them to get to First Republic Bank in downtown Los Angeles as fast as they could. She gave them her cell number and instructed them to call her as soon as they arrive at the branch office. They were on they're way.

It took DA and Dana thirty five minutes to arrive at the bank. DA dialed Ms. Williams's number as they entered the lobby. Ms. Williams answered on the first ring.

"We're in the lobby Ms. Williams," DA informed.

"I'll be right out," Ms. Williams replied, ending the call.

Ten seconds later a beautiful older black woman in her mid-forties appeared in the lobby scanning the patrons. She made a bee line for DA and Dana sitting in a corner. She stood in front of them, staring, long and hard as she could before tears began forming in her eyes.

"Ms. Williams?" DA asked, extending his hand as he and Dana stood to greet the woman.

Ms. Williams hugged both of them like a python, placing kisses on their cheeks. It was a strange occurrence for DA and Dana alike. This unknown woman appeared to have a love for them that seemed almost motherly.

"Come we have a lot to discuss," Ms. Williams ordered, ushering the pair into her office.

Ms. Williams closed her office door and blinds. She stood staring at the pair again. She apologized for losing control of her emotions as tears flooded her face.

"Wow you guys are spitting images of your parents," Ms. Williams said, wiping her face clear of fresh tears.

Ms. Williams began laughing loudly through her tears as she stared at Dana. "You're a beautiful, rough version of you mother."

You knew our parents personally?" Dana asked, smiling at the compliment and leaning forward in her seat.

"Your mother was my best friend," Ms. Williams answered, attempting to dry away a new set of tears. "I've met your parents when we were in Junior High School."

Ms. Williams's memory had taken her back as she shared detail after detail with the two about their parents. How their parents first met and the day they were both born.

DA and Dana wasn't sure if what Ms. Williams spoke was the truth but it flowed effortlessly from her lips. DA and Dana sat attentive to every word that poured from Ms. Williams's mouth.

Dana now understood Ms. Williams's fascination with her. According to Ms. Williams, Dana was her god daughter.

"God daughter?" DA questioned.

"Yes and you're my god son. Because of an accident I had as a young lady I was unable to have children of my own," Ms. Williams explained. "Your parents blessed me to be the God mother of you and Dana. I was there at the hospital when both of you were born. You guys may not remember but I had you guys with me every weekend. I would take you guys everywhere with me. Darryl would have a fit, screaming *if you spoil 'em, you raising 'em,*" Ms. Williams finished, pulling an old photograph from her desk.

Ms. Williams handed the picture to Dana. "See, and I have many more at home."

DA and Dana focused on the picture. They were shocked. It was a picture of them, their parents and a younger Ms. Williams holding Dana in her arms. Of all the old pictures they had seen of their parents and associates, they had never seen this woman in any photograph.

"So Ms. Williams, what does the key go to?" DA asked.

The question instantly brought a sadness to the face of Ms. Williams who was back in deep thought.

"It seems like only yesterday. They were a hell of a couple," Mrs. Williams said, smiling as she recounted. "Darryl was there first and then Diane got hired by the same prosecutor's office."

"Prosecutor's office?" DA questioned befuddled.

"Yes," Ms. Williams emphasized, suspecting the two had not known the truth. "Your parents were District Attorneys working for the Prosecutor's office. That's what the nickname DA stands for, District Attorney not Darryl Arrington. Your parents had you pegged as a District Attorney from the moment they looked at you."

The two sat in amazement as they continued to listen.

"Your parents were making a big name for themselves," Ms. Williams started. "They were taking down a lot of heavy criminals in the underworld. The cops already disliked Darryl and Diane due to virtue of being black and they were proud of it. The first black prominent District Attorney couple, born and raised in South LA, hell yeah they were proud. When the case came across Diane's desk to prosecute a ring of Dirty cops, some of which were the very same officers who openly mocked them, they jumped on it like a shark to blood."

"So our parents were murdered while prosecuting corrupt cops?" Dana asked.

"The day it happened, we all knew who was to blame," Ms. Williams said, fighting back tears again. "No one could ever prove it…it was staged to look like Darryl was drunk and drove off a cliff near Malibu but Darryl never drank, he despised it."

Dana was about to interrupt Ms. Williams when DA signaled by hand gesture to let her proceed.

"Many of our friends were concerned for their safety and we warned them against it," Ms.

Williams spoke. "But once the harassment started, your parents were bent on bringing them dirty cops to justice."

"They were being harassed by the police?" Dana asked.

"Regularly," Ms. Williams indicated with a head nod. The police weren't too happy about an up and coming powerful black couple. Corrupt cops were making indirect threats on behalf of powerful criminals. The top brass of the LAPD were under their scrutiny. They had every reason to be scared and yet they remained fearless."

DA and Dana both smiled, they were proud of learning their parents were fearless.

"What about the key Ms. Williams?" DA inquired, for the second time.

"Do you have the key on you now?" Ms. Williams asked.

"Yeah," Dana answered, producing the key from her pocket.

"Follow me," Ms. Williams instructed the two as she headed out of her office.

DA and Dana followed Ms. Williams into a room. The walls were lined with rows of safety deposit boxes. Ms. Williams walked in and stopped in front of a box and pointed her finger at it.

Dana stepped in front of the box, inserted the key and looked at DA. DA nodded his head and Dana turned the key. Dana pulled the box out of the elongated slot and set it on the table in the middle of the room. She opened the lid. She and DA stood staring at the contents.

They shuffled through the items. Some old cassette tapes secured in a plastic bag, stock and bonds, cash, jewelry, some papers rolled scroll like and a handwritten letter addressed to Darryl Jr. and Dana Arrington.

The two paused as DA held the letter.

"Go head bruh. Open it," Dana encouraged, looking solemn.

DA glanced quickly at Dana, took a deep breath and ripped open the envelope. The letter read:

Our dearest children,

If you are reading this, then we your parents have had the misfortune of not raising you. We love you both with all our hearts and souls. It pains me that I and your father have to make time constructing this letter but we wanted you both to know the truth about our absence from your life. It was not voluntary. I and your father would never want to know a day without our babies.

In the course of justice, we your parents have encountered a threatening evil within the law enforcement of Los Angeles. We aim to rid this city of its wide spread corruption and therefore have been designated a threat.

Your Uncle, James Arrington and God Mother, Deborah Williams have been entrusted to oversee your upbringing. They truly love you two as much as we do. Always show them the kindness and love you would have given us. I hope all that we have prepared and given to you both, will be a blessing to your lives. We look forward to reuniting with our children in the afterlife.

The letter was signed Darryl Sr. and Diane Arrington.

DA, Dana and Ms. Williams all hugged sharing a sea of tears.

"Thank God my babies are home," Ms. Williams whispered, softly kissing them both on the forehead.

DA and Dana hugged Ms. Williams tightly. Neither wanted to let her go. Dana really began sobbing hard. DA wiped away at his face removing the trail of tears streaming down his cheeks. He tried consoling Dana to no avail.

"I've waited all my life to have a mother," Dana spoke, through her sobs holding Ms. Williams as tightly as she could. "I don't ever want to be without you again Ms. Williams."

DA nodded his head in agreement holding Ms. Williams just as tight as Dana.

"You won't Dana," Ms. Williams replied, kissing Dana and DA's head again. "You neither DA. I'll always be here for you both. Now let's get ourselves together. We look a mess," She finished, smiling and elated.

Ms. Williams left the room, returning a short time after with a bag for the contents of the safety deposit box. DA packed the contents and the trio went back to Ms. Williams's office.

The trio exchanged numbers and addresses, promising to stay in touch often. They had set a time for DA and Dana to visit Ms. Williams's home later that day where she would share so many more details and she did.

By the end of the visit to Ms. Williams's home, DA and Dana understood everything clearly.

Their Aunt Betty had only gotten custody because she was listed as kin. She was notified first when Uncle James was murdered, so she arrived in Las Vegas to claim the two children before anyone knew what happened. Aunt Betty too, was desperate to have children but couldn't.

Being the complete opposite of their mother, Aunt Betty didn't take school serious and preferred boys over class. Aunt Betty was diagnosed twice with a sexual disease before the age of fifteen. The court system called her delinquent and ordered Aunt Betty to be sterilized so she couldn't produce what the court labeled "Feeble offspring."

Neither Dana nor DA, knew any of this to be true. What they did know to be true was, Aunt Betty didn't have any children.

Aunt Betty disliked Ms. Williams because of her relationship with their parents. They were closer than most siblings. This explained why Aunt Betty had no pictures with Ms. Williams in it.

Ms. Williams told them Diane and Darryl would never have allowed Betty to raise them if they were alive. Aunt Betty was always high off weed and alcohol. She was barely fit to baby sit and ran after men like a short distance sprinter.

COP KILLAS, JUSTICE SERVED D. MANN

By the time Ms. Williams arrived in Las Vegas the children had been taken into children's custody. Since she was not the biological kin of the children, their whereabouts were not her concerns as far as the courts put it.

Uncle James was murdered after returning to LA one weekend, attempting to garner media coverage on the murder of two District Attorneys. No one would touch the story and his refusal to quit searching for his brother's killer led to his own demise.

Chapter 9

Pocket Rocket

Pockets sat at home watching the news in his living room, he was waiting on the top story to air. Pockets was rolling himself another blunt while he smoked the remainder of a small blunt hanging from his lips.

Pockets kicked his feet up on the table once he finished rolling his blunt. He cozied himself into the corner of the couch and sunk himself in. He could hear keys approaching his door. Pockets knew it was Dana when the key started turning the lock on the front door.

"How'd that meeting go with Ms. Williams," Pockets questioned, as Dana and DA entered the room.

"Beautiful," Dana answered, taking a seat next to Pockets. "She our mother."

"What!" Pockets yelled.

"She our God Mother," DA added, taking a seat in the recliner and sitting the bag on the floor next to the chair.

"Oh. Is that right," Pockets spoke rhetorically. "That's cool, I'm happy for y'all. I just hope it don't blow up in yo' face."

"Why would you say some shit like that," DA questioned, in disbelief.

"Well now that you have another titty to suckle from," Pockets answered, starting the insults. "You subject to really be whining now."

Dana burst out laughing joined by Pockets.

"Nigga fuck you," DA uttered. "Where Crafty at?"

"He went to the store to get something to drink," Pockets responded, still laughing hard. "Imma get you a baby on board sign DA. Titty in da' mouth, titty in da' mouth."

DA smirked the comments off focusing his attention to the top story on the news.

"Oh shit," Pockets said, repositioning his body and pointing to the television. "Nigga check this shit out. Somebody went in hard."

The reporter announced a mystery tale they were calling: *A murder at the Cemetery*.

"Reports were spreading that a family, taking their decease son to his final resting spot were shocked and dismayed to find the son's father lying dead in the grave. Apparently a victim of multiple gunshot wounds," the reporter said. "The victim is believed to be a retired officer from the Newton Division. The Police are investigating this as a definite homicide."

"Somebody operating on a level that's pure fucking genius, pure fucking genius," Pockets said. "I have to give a hat tip to the man. Hat tip."

DA and Dana had nothing to say on the report and instead chose to simply listen. Pockets looked at the two strangely having nothing to say about the death of a cop.

A knock on the door broke the quiet of the moment.

"It's me," Crafty screamed, from the other side of the door.

"It's open," Pockets returned. "C'mon in."

Crafty entered the room acknowledging DA and Dana as he took a seat next to Dana.

"What we sippin' on?" DA inquired, staring at the brown bag Crafty sat on the table.

"The best," Crafty answered, exposing a bottle of Hennessey from the bag. "Here's a cup for everybody."

Crafty poured four cups of alcohol and everyone took their drink.

"So how that meeting go with homegirl?" Crafty asked.

"It turns out that she's our God Mother," DA replied.

"You bullshitting!" Crafty responded, in disbelief.

"Naw homeboy real talk," DA answered. "She was our mother's best friend."

"Wow that's some crazy shit," Crafty added. "Nigga really need a drink on that one."

"You need a drink on everything Crafty," Dana said, laughing and shaking her head.

Pockets turned the television off. The group listened as DA and Dana shared the events concerning their time with Ms. Williams. Pockets and Crafty listened in amazement as DA and Dana told the entire story as their ears had heard it. Surprisingly, neither Crafty nor Pockets had any questions. They listened patiently as they had in court on several occasions.

"I can't believe that shit about Aunt Betty," Crafty said. "I mean…I know she useta' drink but damn, all that other shit. She just seemed so different…so nice."

"Just goes to show how some people can change," Pockets said, philosophizing his point. "It's inevitable, the longer the human mind exist here on earth or what we call age, the more it returns itself to a stage of innocence."

The room was on silence.

"Whadda!" DA interrupted. "Did this negro just dare himself to try and sound intelligent?"

"Nigga you heard me," Pockets cut back in. "the longer yo' ass is here, the more yo' ass is likely to become a soft nigga, a nice nigga. Yeah DA, you…a soft nigga, a nice nigga."

DA pip squeaked his voice mimicking Pockets comments. "You DA…a soft nigga, a nice nigga. Fuck outta here clown!"

DA pulled the bag from the side of the chair and the group began reading through the papers. Some of the papers were dossiers on corrupt officials, cops and gangsters. Some of the papers read like impending charges to be filed against many of the names they now found themselves discussing.

"It's was a bunch of crooks running around this muthafucka back in the days," Crafty said.

"It's a bunch of crooks still running around this muthafucka," DA jumped in.

"Yeah I see," Pockets added. "A lot of these dudes still alive... but this one ain't. This is the cop that just got killed. The one they found in his son's grave," Pockets finished, holding a sheet with Daniel's face on it.

"Let me see," Crafty urged, giving an eye to Dana and DA.

Crafty stared at the picture. It was that bastard alright. Crafty passed the picture to DA while Pockets continued reading the next profile. DA and Crafty were on the same page about keeping the secret from Pockets. Not a word needed to be said, it was understood.

"That's enough of this shit for the night," DA said. "Let me get all this paperwork stuff, I'll skim through this stuff later. Crafty I need to holla' at you outside."

"Hold on DA," Dana halted. "I wanna read through some more of this tonight,"

DA knew Dana's request was about to become a problem. He didn't want her in possession of the paperwork because he knew Pockets would be privy to everything she read.

"We can read this shit tomorrow at my house," DA said, attempting to make light of the situation. "Get some breakfast, a cup of coffee and a fresh start."

"Nigga who said I was going to bed now," Dana questioned, in anger.

"Baby girl, lemme talk to you outside for a minute," DA demanded.

"Naw talk to me right here," Dana ordered, watching DA glance over at Pockets. "Ok. Now I see what's going on. You don't want Pockets to hear. Is that what's going on?"

"This is family business," DA said, stomping out of the house and down the stairs of the front porch. "Dude ain't got shit to do with this."

"Pockets is just as much family as Crafty is," Dana stated, following DA into the garage.

Pockets and Crafty followed the siblings as they continued to argue.

"Just cause' you fucking this nigga don't make him family baby girl," DA returned, spinning around near the back of the garage.

"Hey nigga if you speaking on Pockets gotdammit," Pockets interrupted, crossing the threshold of the garage. "Then you need to address Pockets nigga…like a man nigga, like a man."

DA wasted no time stepping around Dana and into the face of Pockets.

"Is this man enough for you," DA yelled, standing nearly nose to nose with Pockets.

"DA, you need to be removing yo' self from Pocket's face like that," Pockets warned.

"Nigga fuck you," DA screamed, saliva spitting from his mouth. "Do something!"

Pockets felt tiny particles of DA's spittle touch his face. His reaction was swift as his right fist launched forward like a tomahawk missile, crashing DA's chin and sending DA sprawling across the room backwards into the shelves mounted to the garage walls. The shelves broke his fall and DA was back to his feet quickly.

Crafty and Dana rushed to intervene but Pockets was closing in on DA who was now regaining his balance. Pockets threw another punch and DA side stepped it, smashing Pockets right jaw with a solid left straight punch. Pockets tilted like the leaning tower of Pisa. The force of DA's punch sent Pockets from a lean to a full superman dive face first into Aunt Betty's boxes.

Dana and Crafty were now in between the two men. Dana shoved DA backwards screaming at him while Crafty helped Pockets out of the boxes.

"I'm outta here. You can have everything in the bag Dana," DA spoke moving through the garage door. "From here on out, I'm solo."

"Well take this with you," Pockets screamed, breaking free from Crafty and tackling DA outside on the grassy plot in front of the garage.

The two men tussled furiously, trying to strike one another while evading the other's hits. Crafty tried separating the two men with no success. Dana grabbed a loose piece of plywood lying next to the garage and began whooping ass. She struck DA and Pockets several times with the plywood. Both DA and Pockets let each other go and focused on Dana with the stick of wood.

Dana was in a zone. She was kicking ass like an old school grandmamma. Both men jumped to their feet separating from the other, quickly attempting to find distance from the plywood wielding Dana.

"I'm sick of y'all with this bullshit," Dana said, tossing the wood back to the ground. "You niggas stay acting like bitches and here's a news flash for you DA, ain't no solo when it comes to my muthafuckin' family."

"Fuck y'all. I'm outta here," DA announced, walking back to the front of the house.

"Hold on bruh," Crafty urged, catching up to DA.

"Bruh I'm telling you straight up. You tripping," Crafty said, looking DA in the eyes.

"Hold the fuck up," DA yelled, stopping in his tracks. "I know you not taking their side."

"DA, don't even try to play me like that bruh," Crafty stated. "You know muthafuckin' well what's up with me."

DA stood quietly listening to Crafty talk while Dana approached.

"So that's how you feeling big bruh," Dana questioned, approaching DA while Crafty counseled him. "Fuck me huh?"

"Baby girl chill out for a moment," Crafty pleaded.

"Naw Crafty you heard that Nigga," Dana argued. "He said fuck his baby sister. Fuck me! Naw nigga fuck you. I hate yo' ass," Dana finished, walking up the stairs towards the house.

DA heard Dana's comments and charged up the stairs after her. DA pushed his way through the closing door and grabbed Dana by the arm. Dana shrugged her arm trying to free herself from DA's grip.

"Let me go," Dana yelled. "I ain't got shit to say to you DA."

"I'm sorry baby girl," DA started. "I got besides myself. I apologize."

Dana accepted her brother's brief apology. They stood hugging as Crafty and Pockets entered the house.

"Everything cool DA?" Pockets asked, stopping in front of DA.

"Yeah we good bruh," DA responded. "I apologize for spitting in yo' face homie. That was my bad."

"Shit happens when you mad homeboy. It's all good," Pocket said, forgiving DA's actions.

The two men shook hands. This was the first time they had shaken hands since the day they first met.

"Gotta nice little punch on you there," DA complimented, rubbing his jaw.

"Well I didn't appreciate the almost nap in the boxes either but that's a nice right hand you got too," Pockets returned.

"It was the left I caught you with," DA corrected.

"That's how good you caught me," Pockets said, laughing while he massaged his own jaw line. "Nigga wires still a little tangled."

The group sat in the living room laughing along with one another.

"DA, I know you probably gon' be against this idea but whatchu' think about Pockets running with us," Dana asked.

"C'mon baby girl," DA uttered, shaking his head. "You know what's up and you know how I operate. Yo' man, no offense just not suited for this program."

"First of all DA, I don't want to be a part of nothing you got going homeboy. Let's just get that shit clear now," Pockets interrupted. "But whatever you got going that shit got my woman hurt. From here on out, wherever she goes Pockets go."

"The shit might help bruh," Dana added. "You know my man smart."

DA sat staring at the ceiling, swirling his head around with his lips purposely poked out and twisted while completely ignoring Dana statement regarding Pocket's IQ.

"It might be helpful bruh. At worst it's one more pair of eyes watching over baby girl," Crafty urged. "You can't say the youngster ain't quick on his feet."

DA sucked his teeth.

"Nigga he was quick enough to send yo' ass flying across the room while you over there sucking yo' teeth," Crafty said. "And he had enough heart to throw hands with yo' big ass. You can front all you want my nigg but you know that shit gotta count for something."

"Fuck it. That's how both of y'all feel huh. It's his funeral then," DA spoke.

DA stood from his seat and began walking to the door, pulling it open. DA turned at the door facing the group.

"Pockets, it's nothing personal against you but you wild homeboy," DA said, focusing back to Dana and Crafty. "He a loose cannon, he too uncontrollable and he wayyy too trigger happy. It's that kind of shit that fucks up a good plan and gets everybody busted or killed and with that in mind,

I'm against him joining. Don't come crying baby girl when the young brother gets himself killed. Y'all wanted him in."

DA stepped out of the door closing it behind him. Crafty and Dana continued sitting in the living room. Pockets was on his feet before the door could close.

"Pockets can take care of Pockets nigga. Pockets don't need nobody," Pockets yelled, at the door. "Fuck this nigga mean I'm wayyy too trigger happy."

"You are baby," Dana admitted, "You be blazing niggas quickly. You need to chill out."

"I need to chill out!" Pockets screamed. "See! That's what y'all don't know. Why er'body repeating that bullshit talking about," Pockets began mimicking the movements and sounds of a handicapped minor…ugh he ain't take his meds, ugh he on dat' medication," Pockets continued, starting his growl again. "Y'all don't see the mind of a genius. You don't see it, you don't see it. Stop looking cause' it ain't around no more."

"Aww I can't take another word from this nigga right now," Crafty shouted, storming towards the front door. "Maybe you should take yo' meds, it might just make yo' crazy ass chill."

"Naw you tell all those niggas out there they need to chill. Go head! Tell all those niggas they need to chill, don't fuck with Pockets...cause' he's wayyy too trigger happy," Pockets continued, swaying his body back and forth as he emphasized the repeated phrase *wayyy too*. "See what they say. See what they say. They gon' put a shell in yo' fat ass!"

Crafty stepped out of the house and walked over to DA who was now standing at his truck.

"Wassup bruh," Crafty asked. "Why you tripping on the young dude?"

"The young dude hot and hard headed," DA said. "That's a bad recipe for disaster. You can't tell 'em shit."

"Then don't tell 'em. Show 'em," Crafty advised, tapping his forehead. "Thinking man's game homie. Put yo' thinking cap on. Stop letting the anger control you, control it. Guide that young nigga, you know he look up to you. Hell nigga, I look up to you and we both know I kicked yo' ass."

"You wish nigga. I was spanking that ass until you turned into a wrestler on me," DA shot back laughing.

DA couldn't let it go, it was his gut feelings assuring him Pockets would do something uncalled for. Pockets had a history of overly violent type shit. DA couldn't help but smile when he thought *this nigga Pockets is criminal to the max.*

Pockets was only nineteen years old and already a certified killer. The state had already dismissed four murders cases against him due to lack of evidence or witnesses, in just the last two and a half years. The boy was into some gruesome shit too. DA often wondered what happened to him as a child.

Dana and Pockets came out of the house and down the walkway.

"Hey Pockets, if you rolling then you rolling tomorrow," DA exclaimed, kissing Dana on the cheek. "We at the house first thing in the morning baby girl, bring all those papers with you. We got work to do baby girl, it's time for the revenge of the DA's."

DA said his goodbyes and headed off to see Sharon.

Chapter 10

Blood Hound

The media's publicity of the two retired cops killed was spinning the detective's room in a frenzy. Detectives were working overtime trying to solve these cases, it was personal for them too. These murdered officers were decorated members of law enforcement, a family. An honor had been broken. The protection of two of their own had been violated. The perpetrator once caught would suffer a slow death.

Head Detective Jack Barnes sat in his office fumbling through paper after paper on his desk. He was being pressed by the upper echelon of the department to bring a killer to justice fast. The cliché goes, *shit slides downwards on the totem pole* and Jack Barnes was being pounded by ton of it.

These two murdered officers were personal friends of his. Jack was dedicated to closing this case shut…with hot lead.

Looking at the pictures of the deceased made Jack sick. He turned them face down on his desk and yelled out his office for Detective Gomez.

"Yes boss," Gomez replied, stepping in Jack's office.

"Close the door Gomez and have a seat," Jack instructed, leaning back in his chair. "What do we have on our cop killer?"

"Nothing boss outside of ballistics," Gomez reported, looking shamed. "And the ballistics reports are just for Daniel's case. We got detectives questioning everyone from the last thirty years of their lives but nothing solid yet."

"You know Gomez, we might have to set ourselves…" Jack uttered.

The phone ringing interrupted his thought and sentence.

"Hold on Gomez," Jack announced, answering the ringing phone and placing the receiver to his ear. "Yeah hello Jack Barnes speaking."

Jack instantly pulled the phone away from his ear. The first few words through the receiver were curse and swear words. It was the Chief of Police with another pound of shit to drop on Jack's head. Jack remained quiet for the duration of the call. The only words he verbalized were after his greeting were, yes sir.

Gomez wasn't trying to ease drop, the chief was just that loud through the phone. Besides the curse words, the only words distinguishable to Gomez ears were Jack's name, selling snow cones and Alaska.

Jack slammed the phone down back on the hook swearing himself.

"Time is working against us Gomez," Jack exclaimed. "In the event we don't catch our boy in time, we may need a patsy to take the fall. Run through the names and see who looks good for a double murder, we need at least a name we can dangle on the hook," Jack continued, beginning to whisper. "Relieve this pressure from my ass."

"On it boss," Gomez responded, rushing out of the office.

"Schwartz and Kelly," Jack called out. "Get in here."

Moments later the two partners showed up in Jacks office.

"I want you two to start looking for similarities between Daniel Burke's arrest record and John Smith's arrest record," Jack ordered. "See if it's anything we missed."

"Sure boss. We're on it," Kelly responded, and the two partners were off.

Jacks phone began ringing again giving Jack the perfect idea of stepping out of the office for a while. It was time for Jack Barnes to light a fire under somebody. The two things evident in these cases were one, somebody was grinding out a personal vendetta and two; somebody knew something.

Jack was on the lookout for some of his old snitches, maybe the streets had finally heard something. He was listening to anyone who knew of someone capable of killing a cop.

Jack had managed to rouse a few bars and some of its attendees as he worked his way around the city. Truthfully he was going around getting free drinks on the house. Jack knew if he harassed enough patrons, the bar would happily bless him with a couple free shots just to get rid of him.

Jack figured it was time to turn the heat up on local gun dealers. Officer Daniel Burke was killed by handguns out fitted with silencers. This was one item Jack knew wasn't prevalent on the streets. You couldn't get that hard ware off of any corner. This was a specialty.

Jack had a snitch named Sundown. Sundown had been a gun runner since he was young. Jack had collared him twice sending him to prison on both occasions. If anyone knew of specialty hardware being sold, it would be Sundown.

Jack made a quick call on his cellphone requesting a physical address or any address for Sundown. Jack waited on the phone for what seemed the longest minute in history, then the voice came through.

"Ok. I got 'em" Jack stated, placing his cell phone back in his jacket pocket.

Jack had the addresses he needed and was on his way to North Hollywood. Jack had a home address and a work address on Sundown, he would try Sundown's home first and then his job.

Jack pulled up to the address and parked. He could see Sundown loading the back of his truck in his driveway. Jack climbed out of his car and headed up the driveway. Sundown noticed the detective approaching and closed the bed cover of his newer model truck and locked it.

"Sundown! How you doing?" Jack inquired. "What you smuggling?"

"What you want cop?" Sundown replied, with disgust written across his face. "I'm clean, I'm off parole, I work forty plus hours a week at Home Depot and I'm retired from the life. How can I not help you?"

"Sundown! I'm shattered at the level of irreverence you show to a dear old friend such as myself," Jack cried, leaning against Sundown's new truck and folding his arms across his chest. "Truly I must say, I'm appalled. You know I remember a time when you used to love having our special conversations. Boy you could talk a mile a minute back then."

"I don't have a thing for you detective," Sundown declared, opening his truck door.

"We can have this conversation here or we can have it at your job," Jack said, indirectly threatening Sundown's employment. "You know my personal favorite has always been taking assholes like you down to the station, it's a one way trip from there."

"That's the thing I'll always dislike about dirty cops," Sundown started, staring Jack in his eyes. "They never understand any part of the word clean."

"Whew!" Jack taunted, pulling his small note pad from his pocket and scribbling with the tip of his finger. "Let me jot this down as part of my things to learn. Shit! Thanks for the insight convict. I would've been so what...lost without that?"

"You been lost way before I met you cop," Sundown retorted.

"Enough with the pleasantries asshole," Jack uttered sternly. "I wanna know who's selling silencers on my streets. Give me a name now or I start fitting you for two counts of capital murder. I got two dead cops and I don't give a shit who goes down."

"That bullshit will never hold up in court," Sundown spoke, assuredly. "My alibi will have me free within 72 hours."

"Hell I'll take 72 hours. Today on a Monday," Jack announced grinning. "You'll just be getting out early Friday morning."

"I don't know anything cop," Sundown reiterated. "Go harass somebody else."

"I have a better idea," Jack retorted, pulling handcuffs from the small of his back beneath his jacket. "Turn around, place your hands on your head."

"For what cop!" Sundown shouted, turning his back from Jack. "You don't have any cause to arrest me!"

"Wrong asshole!" Jack growled, spinning Sundown around and slamming him against his own truck. "I have the power invested in me to arrest your white trash ass for two counts of conspiracy to commit capital murder."

Sundown heard clicking of the handcuffs Jack were undoing and got very cooperative suddenly. He spent away from Jack screaming his submission.

"Ok! Ok!" Sundown cried out, raising his hands to halt Jack's soon to be actions of cuffing him up.

"Give me a name and I'll vanish like a ghost," Jack suggested.

"Some new guy from Russia, heavy in the mob has been selling hard to get merchandise over the last few months," Sundown spoke, informing Jack of what he knew.

"What's his name?" Jack questioned.

"I don't know," Sundown replied.

"What's the fucker's name before I run your narrow ass in," Jack threatened again.

"I don't know man," Sundown fired back. "It's not like the dude is traveling around passing out his business card ok. Find the Russians, you find him. Ask your FBI friends, I hear they got surveillance on his clique around the clock."

"If I find out you making a mockery out of me; I'll change everything you ever knew about life," Jack warned, putting his handcuffs back in their pouch.

Jack grabbed Sundown's shoulder, shaking it back and forth. "See I knew you would always love these special conversations we have convict."

Jack slapped Sundown's shoulder one final time and strolled down the driveway back to his car.

"You have a good day friend," Jack yelled, from the street, climbing back in his car and driving away.

Sundown gave Jack the middle finger as he pulled away from the curve.

Jack was hoping to have caught a break in the case. If anything Sundown told had half a grain of truth to it, this Russian gun dealer could help possibly identify a cop killer. It was also possible the killer could be Russian and so Jack took the convict's advice.

Jack pulled his phone out of his jacket and started scrolling through his contacts. He pushed the talk button and waited for the phone to start ringing.

"Special Agent Ford speaking," the voice spoke.

"Tim. It's Jack Barnes with LAPD homicide," Jack greeted.

"Hey Jack. How's it hanging over there?" Tim asked.

"It's a shit storm over here Tim," Jack shared. "Two unsolved murders, both ex officers. Haven't had a day's sleep in nearly a week and brass is chewing off what little ass I have left."

"Sorry to hear that. My condolences on your falling brothers Jack," Tim stated. "I heard about it on the news. Let me know if it's anything I can do to help you. You know I'm here for you Jack."

"That's why I'm calling you Tim. I need some information," Jack began. "Anything you can find on a new Russian in town selling specialized hardware. Specifically, pistols and silencers. He may be under surveillance by your department already according to word on the street. This shithead is somehow connected to my killer. I need a name and a location on him ASAP."

"Will do partner," Tim agreed. "I'll give you a call as soon as I have something concrete."

"Thanks a million Tim. I owe you one." Jack told, disconnecting the call and placing his phone back in his jacket.

Jack had a good feeling about this Russian information. He went back to his office to check a few other things he pondered over.

Chapter 11

Fa' Crying Out Loud

The group was at DA's house. They sat around DA's office discussing the new information they had uncovered. DA was trying to match names to faces.

Officer John Smith had leaked a couple names before his demise. DA was sure some of these people had no role in his uncle's death. He wondered if these names played any part in his parent's death. If so, they would all pay for that mistake with their own lives.

DA pulled a picture out of his desk drawer, tossing it on top of the desk. The group took notice of the picture.

"That's our next target," DA announced, to the group. "Watch Commander Jesse Adams."

DA's mind flicked back to the night his Uncle was killed as he stared at the picture of the Watch Commander. His memories were so vivid. He could see it as clear as yesterday. Jesse Adams was one of the men holding down Uncle James when John Smith repeatedly stuck a knife into his body. DA witnessed the entire over kill of his uncle.

They even shot Uncle James at close range in his forehead before leaving his body.

"This bitch ass cop helped to hold our Uncle down while they murdered him," DA stated angrily.

Dana took the picture focusing on it. "So this is one of the bastards that killed my uncle huh? Paybacks a bitch you dead muthafucka."

"I read some of the paperwork y'all parents left," Pockets joined in. "It looks like y'all parents had a gang of dirt on this fool."

"Yeah he was mentioned on a few of those tapes too," Crafty added. "Cracka' was dirty as fuck."

"Cracka still dirty," DA emphasized. "Tonight he paying for his sins though."

The group huddled as DA went over the details of the mission. This guy Jesse Adams was a hard ass even by Police standards, taking him could present a challenge and the group couldn't afford any accidents.

DA understood if he was unable to kill the officers within the time he set for himself, it would be just a matter of time before the cops became aware of his existence. If everything went according to plan, the last officer involved in the deaths of his parents and uncle would be dead before the Police had a clue.

"It's one thing that's been bugging the shit outta me," DA exclaimed, rubbing his fingers against his right temple. "These clowns here were merely foot soldiers taking orders. There's evidence against all of them and a whole bunch of others but nothing indicating the ring leader. I wanna know who was calling the shots."

"I guarantee you one thing. If we torture one of them muthafuckas," Pockets informed the group. "He'll tell us whatever you wanna know…and besides, I got some new shit I wanna try out. Shit'll have 'em hollering like a wolf at the moon."

DA laughed as he took the thought into consideration. He looked at Pockets with a blank stare while in thought. This could be a two for one situation for DA.

DA thought about Crafty's advice from the day before in regards to controlling Pockets.

"Pockets! You say you got some new shit you wanna try out huh?" DA questioned, never taking his eyes off Pockets. "Have 'em hollering like a wolf at the moon?"

Pockets gave his answer with a head nod.

"Looks like we just found you a trial candidate sir," DA announced.

"Yeah buddy," Pockets yelled, unable to contain his excitement. "Imma have his ass talking faster than an auctioneer. One thousand, two thousand, sold to the man with the bloody knife."

"I got the perfect place for you to interview his ass at too," DA uttered, with a partial smile on his face.

"You got your work tools at home Pockets?" DA asked.

"Sure do," Pockets replied.

"Baby girl!" DA called out. "Take Pockets to the house so he can get his tools and get back here soon as possible."

"Crafty! Me and you picking up the garbage later," DA confided.

DA and Crafty sat around for the next hour and a half waiting on Dana and Pockets to return. Crafty was tossing down shots of Hennessey like a professional alcoholic.

"It's about time for you get dressed Crafty," DA suggested, checking his watch for the time.

"Yeah," Crafty agreed, rising from the couch and catching his balance. "Damn I'm buzzing already."

"You smell like a brewery," DA added, as Crafty Disappeared from the room.

DA sipped his drink as he fingered through the papers on his desk. It was possible that he was being over analytical but he felt the mastermind's identity behind his parent's death was right in front of him. There were many names mentioned on the tapes and anyone of them viable.

Dana and Pockets returned. They sat around talking for another ten minutes as they waited for Crafty.

"Damn nigga. You look like you stink," Pockets said, Giving Crafty the once up and down with his eyes as Crafty emerged from the bathroom.

"Shit I feel like it," Crafty said. "Not only do this shit stink but it itch like hell."

"Good," DA interrupted. "It adds to the authenticity. You a bum. You're supposed to stink and scratch."

"That nigga a big ole' homeless black bum," Pockets spoke, laughing loudly.

"Homeless looks good on you Crafty," Dana said, joining in the laughter. "You actually look datable now."

"Dana I need you and Pockets to go get that spot ready," DA insisted. "It's time for me and Crafty to go hunting."

DA loaded up in Crafty's Ford Expedition. Dana and Pockets climbed in her Jaguar and the group left for their destinations.

"Whadda' fuck is that?" Crafty asked, referring to the electronic looking item lying in the middle console. Crafty picked it up, spinning it in his hands. "It look like one of those old school hand held video games."

"It's a Thermal Imager," DA stated flatly.

"A who?" Crafty asked dumbfounded.

"A Ther-mal I-mag-er," DA said slowly, allowing Crafty to read his lips. He could sense Crafty was still in the blind. "It means this piece of equipment can see people through walls based on their body temperature."

"No shit," Crafty said.

"On everything I love," DA swore, stopping the truck and turning the imager on. "Look my nigg."

Crafty watched the screen in amazement as he tried to figure what the heat figures were doing.

"Man how much something like this cost?" Crafty inquired, using the viewer to search room by room.

"A grip," DA replied firmly, squinting his eyes at the screen.

"Hold on my nigg! Is that somebody fucking?" Crafty asked, studying the screen intensely. "Hell Yeah!"

"That's our target. Always on time for some loving," DA added.

"Where you be getting all this shit?" Crafty inquired.

"The internet," DA replied blankly.

"Gotdamn! How much money that internet company of yours make DA?" Crafty questioned.

"This yo' spot right here," DA said, ignoring Crafty's question. "Best be moving, times a wasting."

"Oh like that bruh," Crafty retorted, with a smile placing the imager back in the console and sliding out of the truck. "That's why, I'm not investing in yo' whack ass company."

DA pulled off laughing and headed for his position.

~

Passersby scorned Crafty as he sat on the ground with his back against the building wall begging for spare change.

"Excuse me sir," Crafty called out, tugging the bottom of the man's jacket. "Can you spare the homeless some change sir?"

"Yes I can," the man answered, turning around and squatting in front of Crafty. The man backed his face away from Crafty's, waving his hand back and forth, in front of his face. "Change your address you bum. I see your sorry ass around here again and I'll haul your black stinking ass to jail. Now get lost."

The man stood up and prepared to move on his way when Crafty tugged at the bottom of the man's pants leg.

"Excuse me sir," Crafty repeated. "Can you spare the homeless some change sir?"

"What are you?" The man screamed rhetorically, spinning around in anger and shaking Crafty by his coat collar. "Related to Hellen Keller. What are you deaf, dumb and blind?"

"I'm a veteran sir. I fought for our country," Crafty cried. "Please sir, spare the homeless some change."

The man squatted down in front of Crafty.

"You niggers really are dumb fucks aren't you?" The man started. "We can tell you idiots anything. You idiots didn't fight for YOUR country, you fought for US…white men so that we could dominate your colored world. And guess what nigger, if your black ass makes it home, you're not a hero…No! You're still nothing more than a good nigger. Job well done soldier," The man finished, standing and patting Crafty on top of his head with a hefty laugh.

The man turned to walk away and Crafty grabbed both of the man's ankles, yanking with so much force that the man went crashing to the ground face first. The man was able to shield his face with his hands as he struck the ground. The fall had dazed the man momentarily. The man shook his head, trying to regain his composure.

The man's sight was still blurry when he peeked to the side and saw the bottom of DA's big black boot stomping his head into the pavement. The man was knocked out cold.

~

"What's taking this dude so long," DA asked, glancing down at his watch. "We ain't got all day."

"He getting dressed," Dana replied.

"Tell this dude to hurry up man," DA advised.

"Give 'em a minute," Dana demanded. "He'll be out."

No sooner than DA could sigh Pockets entered the room dragging his roll along luggage case.

"Whadda," Crafty whispered. "I thought my costume was bad."

DA and Dana turned around taking notice of Pockets attire.

"Whadda!" DA shrieked.

Pockets strolled across the shop as the group stared on with open mouths.

Pockets wore what looked to be a full body snorkel suit covered by jean overalls. Pockets sported a pair of long yellow rubber gloves that he taped off at his biceps and a pair of rubber boots that came to his thighs. With the snorkel suit covering Pocket's head, it was anyone's guess to why Pockets was donning a clear shower cap on top. The pair of goggles Pockets wore were so foggy from steam, DA couldn't see his eyes as he approached him.

Pockets couldn't hear DA calling as he bobbed his head to the music he was listening to. DA waved, grabbing Pocket's attention. Pockets pulled out one of the ear buds stopping to hear DA. DA smiled giving Pocket's the once over visually.

"I need that muthafucka in there singing!" DA emphasized.

"Don't worry bruh," Pockets assured, placing his ear bud back in his ear and continuing with his head bop. "Better than Ron Isley."

Pockets walked into the room where Jesse was being held cuffed to a steel frame that was mounted securely to a wall. He left his luggage case sitting in the middle of the floor as he walked over grabbing the unconscious Jesse's chin and turning his face side to side.

"Jesse Adams!" Pockets yelled, slapping blood out of Jesse's mouth. "Wake yo' punk ass up nigga. You got some singing to do homeboy."

Pockets turned around to retrieve his luggage and noticed the group standing in the doorway with eager eyes. He approached them, ushering them backwards.

"Pockets can't work with a crowd staring over his shoulders," Pockets said grabbing the door and swinging it slowly closed. "He don't operate like that!"

The door closed and the group went back to sitting around the metal shop. Dana who had already finished rolling a blunt was putting the smoke in the air. The group sat back quietly rotating the blunt between them, waiting to hear screams or pleading from Jesse. It was silent.

Five minutes had passed before the group started hearing the first moans and groans of Jesse. The loud whining cry startled the group as they spent around in their seats, focusing on the door.

The cries turned into constant full screams and then back to whimpering as the group listened.

"Ah-ah-aaahhhh," Jesse screamed, over and over again.

Pockets open the door and came out holding an empty jug.

"I need somebody to fill this jug with water," Pockets requested.

Crafty was on his feet quickly and heading for Pockets standing in the doorway. Crafty reached for the jug as he tried to peer over Pocket's head to spy a look.

"Bruh you don't even wanna see," Pockets warned, shaking his head no and pushing his hand against Crafty's chest.

"Shiiid," Crafty harmonized. "Yes the fuck I do!"

"It's yo' stomach my nigg," Pockets replied, side stepping Crafty. "Don't say I didn't warn you."

"Nigga I dun' seen worst," Crafty Argued.

Crafty peered in the room, noticing the table set up similar to a laboratory. He was stunned. Pockets had a full chemistry set up on the table, complete with brewing potions and the whole nine. Crafty glanced over at Jesse and his stomach dropped. Crafty bent over hurling the contents of his stomach to the floor. He backed out the room looking sick.

"Crafty!" DA yelled, him and Dana jumping to their feet. "You alright my nigg?"

"That nigga Pockets is sick homeboy," Crafty indicated, huffing and puffing on the verge of another stomach eruption.

"Man can I get another bottle of water fa' this muthafucka die on me," Pockets insisted, watching DA and Dana sit Crafty down in a chair.

"Hey that fat nigga alright," Pockets yelled. "The muthafucka in here is the one about to die. Now can I please get some water?"

Pockets tossed the empty container over to Dana. Dana rushed over to the sink to fill the bottle. DA decided to have a look for himself. DA walked over to the door where Pockets was still standing guard.

"Don't do it," Pockets warned.

DA peeked over Pocket's shoulder. One look at Jesse and DA was covering his own mouth trying to avoid his own stomach eruption.

"Damn homie! Is he alive?" DA questioned skeptically.

"Yeah," Pockets replied nonchalantly. "Pain knocked 'em out."

DA stared at Jesse again, turning his focus to Pockets. Jesse's clothes had been torn from him. A rather large puddle of blood formed beneath Jesse's feet. Pockets had made a bunch of tiny incisions across Jesse's body and face which were bleeding slowly.

In some spots Pockets had simply cut pieces of flesh off of Jesse's body, letting them fall to the floor. The tip of Jesse's nose, a part of his ear and a couple fingers laid on the floor amidst the bloody mess. Jesse also had numerous burns over his body. From the looks of things, Pockets was starting to cut open the bottom of his stomach.

Dana brought the water and tried to peek in the room. DA caught her advancement and stopped her.

"Hell naw you can't look in there," DA opposed. "You sleep with that nigga."

Pockets took the water and closed the door. DA and Dana returned to Crafty.

"Man that nigga got some serious issues," Crafty spoke, shaking his head.

"I know one thing. After that shit there, dude should be ready to tell Pockets everybody's name in the department," DA uttered, with a slight chuckle.

"Fire that blunt back up baby girl," Crafty asked. "That shit fucked off my high."

"Mines too," DA added.

The group sat smoking when the screaming started again, this time they could hear Jesse's pleas.

"For crying out loud," Jesse pleaded. "Kill me already."

The screams subsided momentarily before they returned louder and with more desperation. As quick as the screams had come, they were now gone. Pockets came out of the room disrobed of his shower cap and gloves.

"He all yours DA," Pockets exclaimed.

"What he say?" DA asked.

"He said the chief was calling shots. He was a captain back then," Pockets told.

DA thought about it logically and it made sense. The chief was under investigation back then from Internal Affairs, the prosecutor's office and the Justice Department. It seems, the then Captain was a wanted man. No one could ever stick a case on him though and he advanced through the ranks to where he is today.

"Go ahead and finish that cop off Pockets," DA ordered, peeking in the room again. "Shit he look dead already."

"Give me a pistol," Pockets demanded. "I'll close his eyes for good."

DA handed Pockets his pistol and Pockets walked back into the room. A second later a single shot was heard and Pockets reemerged from the room.

"One to the head," Pockets spoke, scanning the group's faces. "Now who gon' help me clean this shit up?"

"C'mon. Me and Crafty will help you," DA agreed reluctantly, starting to feel sick again. "Dana go see moms and ask her about the captain, soon to be ex-chief."

Dana took off and the group went about the business of cleaning the place up.

They wrapped Jesse's body in plastic, burning the plastic sealed. Pockets had mixed special chemicals he claimed would annihilate any DNA evidence from the scene. This was some shit he claimed to have watched on a show called "How to get away with murder.

Pockets sprayed the chemical covering the entirety of the blood stains. He grabbed the fire extinguisher off the wall, sat it down between his feet and pulled a book of matches from his pocket.

Pockets struck a match and tossed it at the blood stains mixed with chemicals. The blue flame quickly engulfed the stains on the floor, traveling up the brick wall with the metal frame that Jesse was attached too.

"Whoa!" DA sighed, looking at blue flame.

Pockets grabbed the extinguisher quickly putting the flame out.

"That's enough," Pockets exclaimed. "The blue flame helps to alter the molecules of the blood once it mixes with the chemicals. That's why the building doesn't burn down cause' it's a blue flame and even if they found a drop of blood, they could never analyze it for DNA. You can learn a lot watching those TV crimes shows."

As far as DA was concerned, Pocket's last comment solidified his spot as a true idiot. DA knew that entire story was some made up bullshit, he wasn't sucking that shit up with a straw.

Crafty backed the van to the bay door and blew the horn. The group loaded up Jesse's deceased body in the rear of the van and Crafty took the body to dump it.

Chapter 12

No Brown Nosing

Detective Jack Barnes sat at his desk frustrated. Another officer had been found murdered.

The discovery of Officer Jesse Adams's body wrapped in plastic on the freeway had the Chief of Police calling Jack Barnes in a rage.

"You either solve this case in the next 72 hours or you'll be washing police cruisers at the academy dammit!" The Chief screamed, slamming the phone in Jack's face.

"Brown! Get in here," Jack yelled, out of his office door.

"Yes Sir," Brown replied, stepping in the doorway.

"Black coffee, two sugars," Jack insisted, eyeing her hips as she stood in the doorway.

Officer Brown rolled her eyes as she turned and walked out of Jack's office.

She was tired of being his personal pet. Of all the detectives in the room, she noticed she was the only detective never assigned to any important cases. In fact, she was only called when it came to servicing the other detectives. She was beyond tired of being the errand girl of the division. She was the youngest black woman in the history of her precinct to make detective. Sharon wasn't about to let herself be devalued.

Officer Brown stood at the coffee machine preparing a foam cup with three sugars. She had a quick thought, *for each and every one of you racist perverts.* With a quick check of the squad room, she allowed a dribble of spit to fall in the coffee pot. She swirled the coffee inside the pot before she poured it in the cup.

"Here you go sir," Officer Brown said, placing the cup of coffee on Jack's desk with a false smile.

Officer Brown secretly despised her colleagues. She had been sexually harassed since her first day at the academy. She was keen to the eyes that followed her body wherever she walked. She had every sexual advancement known to women, thrown at her in her first week of training.

"Brown close the door and have a seat," Jack instructed.

Officer Brown was ready for the usual sexual harassment as she took a seat.

"Brown you're a good officer. You're one of the few dependable officers in this squad room and that's a plus for you," Jack said, with his eyes planted directly on her breast. "Have you put any thought to advancing your career?"

"No sir. I'm perfectly content in my current position," Brown answered, feeling the disgust that often smothered her when she attended work.

Jack rose from his chair, walked over and took a seat on the edge of his desk.

"I have to promote someone from this squad," Jack started. "This could be a good thing for you, if you want it."

"Like I said before sir," Brown responded. "I'm content with my current position."

"You sure about that? With the death of Adams, there's a lead detective spot open now," Jack stated, leaning closer to whisper in Brown's ear.

Brown closed her eyes and gritted her teeth as she tried to block out the lewd proposition being whispered in her ear.

"Is that all sir!" Brown said, rising from her seat in disgust.

"Yeah. That's it for now," Jack replied, looking sinister. "Give me a call at home if you wanna discuss that promotion."

Brown left Jack's office irate inside, she was boiling hot. She took a seat at her desk, scanning the squad room. *All of you nasty ass racist will pay dearly* she thought to herself. Every man in her eye sight was guilty.

Brown couldn't stand another moment in that squad room and decided to clock out early.

Officer Sharon Brown sat in her personal car allowing her tears to fall unrestricted from her eyes. She was in debate with herself. Should she resign and find another job or should she stay employed as a cop. She needed someone to talk to fast. She knew just who to go to.

Officer Brown pulled her phone from her pocket, called a number and waited.

"Hey you busy right now?" She asked, when a voice answered the phone.

The voice on the other end of the phone was a comforting one. She smiled as she indicated her time of arrival at his destination. The voice assured her that he would be waiting on her.

Sharon blew her horn as she pulled in the driveway and parked. DA stood in the doorway as she climbed out of her car and approached the porch.

"Hey Babe," Sharon whispered, in DA's ear as she hugged him tightly. "How you doing?"

"I'm good," DA responded, leaning backwards to observe Sharon's face. "Everything alright with you? You don't look too good."

The thought of her workplace brought instant tears to her eyes as she fell back into DA's chest sobbing.

"C'mon in and have a seat," DA instructed, the distraught woman.

He knew what her problem was, it was that job. Sharon had bitched about her job from the moment he met her. It was always the same complaint.

"You want a drink or something?" DA offered.

"Naw I'm cool. Thank you," Sharon replied, following DA to the couch. "I just needed someone to listen."

"In that case I'm all ears," DA replied, taking a seat next to Sharon and caressing her hands with his own. "Whenever you ready."

"I'm so tired of that damn job DA. Every...fucking...day I got one of these racist, kill a nigga cops, trying to get my black ass in his bed," Sharon told. "They can't stand black men but they'll fuck every black woman on the planet, you know. Shit makes me sick. I swear I feel like killing all of them racist fucks."

DA didn't say a word, he continued to listen.

"Today my superior calls me in his office. I knew it was bullshit when he called my name," Sharon spoke, showing the face of someone truly disgusted. "Nasty devil can never take his eyes off my body. The whole time he talking to me, he staring right at my breast," Sharon paused, taking a deep breath. "I'm sitting in this devil's office while he's trying to gas me up with this sudden promotion thing, you know. This lead detective in the unit got killed, his spot is open. Fuck 'em. He was a racist dick too."

DA didn't say a word, he continued to listen.

"He sits up on the edge of the desk and I tell myself, *here it comes, brace yourself girl.* This fucker leans over and whispers in my ear, that if I suck his dick, he'll guarantee me the promotion of lead detective. I swear I thought about tasering his little pink, alien dick ass."

DA didn't say a word, he continued to listen.

"Believe it or not," Sharon continued. "I believe that's the reason, why so many women who work there, either turn lesbian (mostly butch), quickly find a husband in the department because cops aren't so quick to test other cops or we suffer silently. Anything beats those devils…just…fucking you and then fucking over you, figuratively."

DA sighed the word *Hmmm* and continued to listen. He thought about his sister in that moment.

"I've even had a couple sisters warn me not attend any of their…," Sharon paused, setting her two quote fingers with both hands, besides her head. "Rape parties."

DA didn't say a word, his head jerked back. He was stunned.

"Yeah. Rape parties," Sharon told. "A house party style get together with most of the top ranking officers in the department. The new officers, I mean fresh meat is invited, quickly liquored up pass the point of sobriety and then fucked senseless by nearly every male officer there. If the women ain't wit' it, they're indirectly warned to never let their name appear on a complaint. I ain't never been to one and I ain't never going."

DA allowed Sharon to express herself uninterrupted until she got quiet, staring DA down. Sharon felt a little relief now after expressing herself. She needed DA to relieve the rest of her. DA guided her by hand, upstairs to his bedroom.

Chapter 13

Game Changer

Dana couldn't wait to share the new information she had learned while talking to Mama Williams. Now Dana had the entire story. Ms. Williams remembered so much more at the mentioning of the Chief of Police, formerly known as Captain Dale Harris.

Captain Dale Harris was as dirty as they came. The man escaped more prosecutions than Houdini in his days. He was facing some hard time until the cop who turned state's evidence and a witness both went missing the day before trial started. Both men turned up dead the next day, their bodies discovered laying in the LA River.

There were no questions of who and why these men were killed, everyone knew. Dale Harris had ordered the hit and his pit bull Jack Barnes carried it out. No one could ever prove anything on either of them but it was well known in the right circles exactly what happened.

Dana pulled over and parked in front of DA's house. She wondered who black Dodge Charger sat in her brother's driveway.

Dana slid out of her car and approached the door.

"DA!" Dana yelled, ringing the doorbell relentlessly. "DA!"

DA opened the door and Dana stepped inside.

"Good Morning baby girl," DA greeted, walking to his kitchen.

"Good Morning bruh," Dana replied, following DA through the house.

"So whatchu' find out from moms yesterday?" DA asked.

"I know who killed our parents," Dana responded. "Some cop name Jack Barnes."

"Jack Barnes?" Sharon questioned, walking in on the end of the comment. "That's the name of my superior I told you about last night DA."

"We discussing someone with the same name," DA responded. "Sharon this is my sister Dana. Dana this is Sharon."

The two women greeted one another with pleasantries. Everyone took a seat at the kitchen table.

"Sharon. So how long have you been seeing my brother? If you don't mind me asking," Dana questioned, shaking her head at DA and swiftly changing the topic. "My brother loves to hide everything from me."

"No I don't mind," Sharon answered. "I've been seeing DA for almost a month now and it's been the best month I've had in a long time."

"One month!" Dana yelled. "Damn DA, when were you planning to introduce me to your girlfriend?"

"In about never," DA answered, ignoring Dana's theatrics and returning the warm smile Sharon gave him.

"So DA, what do you have planned for the day," Sharon asked. "I refuse to go into that place today. One more indirect sexual reference from anyone in that squad room and I'm gon' open fire in there."

Dana's head jerked back. "Whoa! Hold up! Back up! You a cop?"

"Yeah. A detective," Sharon answered, smiling. She knew what most black people thought of cops. Sharon was black and felt no differently now herself.

"Now that's a game changer," Dana fired off. "If I ever heard one."

"Don't mind my sister," DA warned. "She kinda special."

"And you a special kind of stupid," Dana retorted. "You know that DA?"

"It's cool," Sharon urged. "I get that a lot when I tell people my occupation."

"DA I have a confession to make," Sharon spoke, giving him time to prepare for the impending news.

"A confession already," Dana interrupted. "Damn, I feel one of those Usher moments coming on."

"Shut yo' ass up Dana," DA warned. "Continue Sharon."

"The day we met, you told me that you didn't have anything to hide." Sharon started. "I was trained as a cop DA, it's in me! I ran a background check on you. I'm sorry DA for the invasion of privacy but curiosity got the better of me. I wanted to know who I was about to deal with."

DA and Dana listened attentively as Sharon talked.

"You knew who I was didn't you?" Dana questioned Sharon.

"You're his only next of kin," Sharon confessed.

"I knew it. It was the way you looked at me before we shook hands," Dana interrupted. "You looked at me like you knew me from somewhere."

"Case files girl," Sharon responded, bursting out in laughter. "And I see your name has been mentioned once or twice."

Sharon considered Dana to favor the rap star known as Da' Brat. She admired the beautiful yet rough and strong side of Dana.

"But what I want to tell you DA, well both of you since you're both here," Sharon rested, taking a deep inhale.

"Y'all have to promise on y'all lives to never tell where y'all got this information from," Sharon insisted, looking overly concerned. "If it ever gets out that I told y'all, I'm a dead woman!"

"I don't know what you about to tell us Sharon," Dana interrupted again. "But I do know people don't risk their lives for nothing. So why? And whatchu' want out of it?"

"I'll tell you what now," Sharon replied, staring DA straight in the eye. "I'll tell you why and what I want out of it, at the end of this story."

DA didn't say a word, he nodded his head and simply listened.

"Alright, let's hear it," Dana agreed.

"While I was researching your background I ran across some stories about your parent's death," Sharon disclosed, watching neither of the two blink.

"I won't lie, I was shocked to learn they we're district attorneys here in Los Angeles. What shocked me more is that right before their death, they were investigating some of the cops still working in my precinct," Sharon voiced. "Immediately, I started researching day' asses. Once I read through their archives, I was disgusted to see these muthafuckas still had a job. I got pissed when I thought about how they got promoted after all the crimes they'd committed. Every one of them muthafuckas should have been on death row for just for the shit they were suspected of. Y'all parents were about to slam the gavel down, for life."

DA nor Dana said a word. They listened.

"This is where it gets real interesting. The lead detective investigating your parent's death was none other than my current superior officer Jack Barnes," Sharon revealed. "Which happens to be one of the cops your parent's had under investigation. Back then, Jack Barnes took all his orders from another man under your parent's scrutiny…the now chief of police, Dale Harris. Also it's a good chance that y'all uncle was murdered by these same dirty cops in my unit."

DA and Dana sat quietly eyeing one another.

"Ok, so we've heard the what part now," Dana interjected. "What's up the why and what you want out of it part?"

Sharon was a little shocked, she was expecting more of a reaction from the two.

"The why and what I want out of it is simple," Sharon spoke. "I wanna help the man that I love to avenge his family and I want him to understand how loyal I will always be to him. DA I love you and I wanted to thank you for making my ugly life so beautiful over this last month. You're incredible."

Dana quickly spoke the word "bullshit," through a hard, fake cough.

DA smiled as he nodded his head in approval. He trusted her words. Dana also trusted her words. Dana reached over hugging Sharon.

"Sharon, please don't tell his big head ass nothing like that again," Dana said, flashing the brightest smile ever. "He already think he da' shit."

"That's my king Dana," Sharon added, with her own smile. "I'll do whatever he tells me to."

DA rose from his chair, leaning over to kiss Sharon on the lips.

"I have an errand to run. I'll be back in an hour," DA stated. "Dana...**talk** to Sharon while I'm gone."

"Talk to her, talk to her," Dana emphasized, with uncertainty.

"Yeah. Talk to her, talk to her," DA reiterated, with certainty placing his hand on her chin. "She rolling with her king now."

Sharon smiled feeling the love from DA. It was something she had been wanting for a while, to feel loved and accepted.

DA got dressed for the day leaving Dana and Sharon alone to talk.

Chapter 14

Barnes Storming

Detective Jack Barnes sat at his desk rumbling through pictures and files of John Smith, Daniel Burke, Christopher Burke and Jesse Adams. Christopher was the only civilian of the group. It was Christopher's death that caused Jack so much confusion. What was the meaning of his death?

Jack continued to rumble through what little evidence he had and then it hit him like déjà vu. This was the old click, minus Christopher, himself and the chief. There had been no attempts on his or the chief's life but Jack felt the old crew might present his best lead yet.

Jack leaned back in his chair and started to reminisce about the old crew. The crew caused a lot of havoc in its hay day. The crew had fucked over so many people, Jack knew any number of people could have been gunning for any member of that click. The entire crew was dirty from head to toe.

"Brown! In my office now," Jack called out.

"She didn't come in today boss," Gomez said, suddenly appearing in Jack's doorway.

"Bring me everything you can find on Detective Jesse Adams," Jack ordered. "And a cup of black coffee."

"Sure boss," Gomez obliged, disappearing from the door as quick as he had come.

Jack recalled the visit from Daniel a few days prior. Daniel was sure that the police were overlooking something. *Maybe Daniel was right* Jack thought to himself as he poured through the information on his desk. It was worth a shot to recheck.

Jack began thinking back to the numerous cases where they had screwed someone over. They had killed and planted so much evidence on so many people, Jack knew he had his work cut out for him. This would be a tedious search but it needed to be done quickly. The chief was still breathing down his ass.

Jack's office phone started to ring. He picked up the receiver and placed it face down on the desk. Jack wasn't in the mood for conversation today, especially not from the chief of police.

Jack reached in his desk, retrieving a bottle of Vodka. He removed the top and took a big gulp of the alcohol. He placed the bottle back in the drawer and closed it.

Jack stared out of his office window while he pondered. He thought about the vodka burning his throat on the way down. The gulp of vodka gave him his next thought. It was time to pay the Russians a visit.

Jack got up and headed out of the precinct. He knew just who he wanted see, Alexander Anasenko. The little shithead had run and escaped Jack the day before.

Alexander Anasenko, wanna be Russian mobster who didn't have any of what it takes to become a mobster. Alex was a stone's throw from being a junkie. Jack had busted Alex a couple of times doing petty crimes to get accepted in the family. Jack released him on a promise that when he called, Alexander better answer.

Jack passed the Red Hammer Club in downtown Los Angeles. The place was crawling with Russian mobsters. Jack made a U-Turn pulling in front of the club. He hopped out and approached the two men blocking the door.

"Private club!" The Russian exclaimed, extending his large arm and hand to signal stop.

"Not anymore," Jack replied, pulling the bottom of his jacket, enough to expose his badge and gun.

The two Russians in front of the door didn't budge. The other Russians who stood around conversing were now gathering around Jack.

"Fuck your badge!" One of the Russians blurted out.

"And fuck you cop!" Yelled another.

"If you boys wanna do this the hard way. I can have fifty cops down here, tearing this place apart before you get a chance to say to your boss with that dumb ass look on your face," Jack said, giving his best impersonation of a Russian idiot. "I didn't know he just wanted to ask a simple question boss."

The men glanced at one another confused about what to do.

"Your move dopey," Jack antagonized.

The men cleared a pathway and Jack entered the club mumbling something about foreigners.

The club was packed with party goers as Jack made his way through the crowd. Jack headed to the back of the club where he could normally find the junkies there, half passed out against a wall or something. Alex could always be found hanging out among the rejects.

Jack stopped in the middle of the floor, scanning the upper levels of the club. He spotted the Russian boss, Viktor Sokoloff guarded by his cronies and preceded to the stairwell. Jack was about to give Viktor a proper welcome back.

Jack walked up the stairs, once again being accosted by Russians foot soldiers. Jack pulled his badge, holding it high for the boss to see. "I'm the law in this goddamn town. Anybody have a problem with this?"

"What do you want?" The boss questioned, waving Jack through.

"I'll tell you what I don't want Viktor," Jack answered, taking a seat across the table from the boss. "I don't want disease like you in my town...and I really don't care to be in your presence now," Jack continued, taking a brief glance around. "It reminds me of a rodent infestation."

"You detectives come into my legal place of business throwing around insults," Viktor replied. "Never once, uttering a word of respect. Why should I concern myself with the likes of you?"

"It's a little thing here in America, called law Viktor," Jack started out, pouring himself a shot of their vodka. "I can't say I love it, it's kind of a shitty system. However, I do love enforcing it. It gives to me, the exclusive right to deal with shitheads like you any…fucking…way I see fit," Jack continued, swallowing the shot of vodka. "Like now for instance, I come for a simple answer but do I receive the red carpet treatment," Jack continued, slapping himself on the chest while asking the rhetorical question. "Oh no! I'm greeted by two sub human steroids with apparently the combined IQ of a newborn. I could take this visit here as disrespectful, after all you haven't uttered a word of respect yet."

"What do you want from me cop?" Viktor asked.

"A name. I want to know who bought several pistols from you equipped with silencers. Silencers that just so happen to be used in the murder of a cop," Jack demanded. "A name Viktor."

Jack scanned the club as he waited for Viktor's response. He caught a glimpse of Alex and a woman on the lower level, heading towards the back of the club in a hurry.

"You assume too many things about me cop," Viktor retorted, counting down one finger on his raised hand as he laughed. "One, you assume I care about a dead cop, I don't. Two, you assume that I would admit to the selling of any kind of weapon. I don't again and I didn't. Three, you assume that I would give you the names of my most valuable customers. I will not. So cop it looks as if we have a stalemate."

Jack smiled at Viktor and Viktor smiled back.

"For now," Jack agreed, rising from his chair and walking back towards the stairs. "Maybe next time Viktor."

Jack walked down the stairs and headed to the back. He entered the men's and women's restrooms, checking stall by stall. Alex was in neither. Jack headed for the back door.

Jack opened the back door and there Alex stood with the women, huddled in a corner snorting coke. Jack approached quietly from behind.

"There you go you little piss poor excuse of a human," Jack shouted, grabbing Alex by the back of his coat collar and raising him to his toes. "Turn around you maggot."

Alex and the woman were both screaming to the top of their lungs. Jack delivered a powerful punch to the stomach of Alex causing him to drop to his knees. The woman attacked Jack, slapping the hell of his head. Jack spent around smacking the woman and sending her sprawling into a trash can.

"The next time I ask you for a name, you better damn well give it to me," Jack threatened, applying another gut punch to Alex.

"I say take your filthy hands off him," Viktor screamed, standing behind Jack with six of his foot soldiers.

Jack turned around, surprised by the number of men and how close they were to him.

"This is official police business. Back the fuck up!" Jack growled, as the men continued to make his circle smaller. "Back the fuck up!"

Jack pushed Alex into the group of men and tried to grab for his gun. One of the Russian men grabbed for his gun simultaneously ripping the gun from Jack's hand. Another Russian grabbed Jack's left arm and Jack was pulled as if he was hanging on a cross. The Russians pounded Jack's mid-section and face. Jack was hurled to the ground by another huge Russian and the group took turns kicking Jack around the alley like a soccer ball.

Jack's weapon was emptied of its bullets and thrown at his head as he laid in his own bloody mess.

"Next time show a little more respect for the culture of others when you enter their place of business," Viktor warned. "Or this could become a pattern of life for you. I suggest you not show your face around here again cop, you won't be so fortunate again."

Chapter 15

Skeletons Coming to Haunt

It was five minutes until quitting time when Officer Sharon Brown strolled into Jack Barnes office.

"I didn't call you," Jack spoke.

Sharon closed the door and blinds and slid Jack a piece of paper with a location on it.

"Be there in exactly one hour," Sharon insisted.

"What's this about?" Jack questioned.

"It's about my promotion," Sharon whispered, leaning over Jack's desk placing her mouth next to his ear. "Only I won't be sucking your tiny dick sir but you will be kissing this big beautiful black ass."

"I don't know what makes you think you're going to receive a promotion," Jack responded, with a slight laugh that caused pain in his rib cage. "Not without me authorizing it."

"Not only will I receive a promotion. I'm gon' be held as a hero when I solve the case of the cop killer single handedly," Sharon retorted.
"Everyone will want to know how you veteran

cops missed the lead of a lifetime and how this rookie detective solve the case. I promise to be modest when I give my answer Jack."

"If you have information pertinent to this case Officer Brown, I command you to hand it over," Jack scolded. "That's an order."

"Fuck you Jackie," Sharon returned. "You got one hour before I make you look stupid in front of this department and the entire police organization. Be there!"

Sharon turned around grabbing the door knob. She paused and turn to look at Jack one more time.

"What a fucking mess you created Jack," Sharon voiced. "Your skeletons are coming back to haunt you."

Sharon walked out of Jack's office feeling vindicated. She knew she had his attention. She relished in the moment.

Jack memorized the location and destroyed the paper. With a quick inspection of his gun Jack was on his way out of the office.

It was exactly one hour later when Jack pulled up to the location he had memorized. It was a house. A white couple sat on the porch watching the sun go down. The house seemed eerily familiar to

Jack. Sharon pulled along the side of Jack and rolled her window down.

"This house should ring a bell with you Jack," Sharon said. "This is where it all started."

Jack stared at house drawing a blank.

"Nothing yet huh?" Sharon inquired. "Don't worry it'll hit you by time we get to the next location. You're going to love this one. Follow me Jack and make sure to keep up."

Sharon rolled her window up and gunned her engine up the block. Twenty minutes later she was pulling into an industrial section of Inglewood, California. Jack pulled in behind her.

Sharon got out of the car and ushered for Jack to follow.

"Did you figure out the house yet Jack?" Sharon questioned, walking between the buildings.

Jack smirked, he didn't have an answer.

"It belonged to Darryl and Diane Arrington," Sharon said, pausing in time to witness Jack's eyes widen as large as aliens eyes.

"C'mon Jack let's go," Sharon urged, starting her move again.

Jack was blindsided by that information. His mind flooded with old thoughts of the Arrington's. He followed Sharon to a metal works shop according to the sign on the front of the building.

"What's this?" Jack questioned.

"This is where I found MY first piece of physical evidence," Sharon replied, picking the lock with professional tools.

Sharon and Jack entered the establishment.

"Follow me Jack," Sharon ordered, leading the way to a room near the back.

Sharon opened the door and turned on a light switch.

"Well what do you see?" Sharon asked.

"Metal," Jack answered.

"Look over here," Sharon said, walking over to brick wall with a metal frame mounted to it.

"It looks like someone burned the wall," Jack noted, the incident in his mind. "And what the hell are all those stains?"

"My guess," Sharon speculated. "It's blood. It appears as if someone attempted to cover up the blood splatter by burning the stains."

Jack nodded his head in agreement. He was impressed so far but he wouldn't let Sharon know it.

"This is all good rookie but I ain't seen no physical evidence yet," Jack commented.

"That's because I haven't shown it to you yet," Sharon replied, pulling a small evidence baggie from her front shirt pocket and placing it in her hand. "What we have here is one piece of torn shirt belonging to no other than Detective Jesse Adams. Forensics confirmed it already."

"You ran this through forensics?" Jack asked.

"Sure did. Nice and quietly too," Sharon responded. "The blood stains on the floor; this is where Jesse Adams was killed."

Jack and Sharon both stood staring at the enormous stains. Jack felt saddened and depressed, Sharon felt elated.

"I'll have forensics comb this room tomorrow for any more evidence I may have missed," Sharon stated.

"Tomorrow! Why not tonight?" Jack ascertained.

"I'm catching a killer tonight Jack," Sharon countered, checking her watch for the time. "Well

Jack this is where we part. I have a killer to bring to justice."

Sharon walked out of the room on her way back to her car. Jack pursued her.

"Wait a minute! Wait a minute dammit!" Jack screamed. "Ok run me down on what you got and let's talk about that promotion of yours."

"I gotta better idea Jack," Sharon said, getting ready to play hard ball. "Let's talk about that promotion first and then MAYBE...I'll run you down on what I know or you can watch it all play out on the morning news; starring yours truly."

"You got yourself a deal," Jack agreed. "Now give me the full run down."

"I can't right now. I'm running late to catch a killer," Sharon spoke.

"I'm riding with you then," Jack said. "You can fill me in on the way."

Sharon told Jack half of the truth, just enough to get his mouthwatering. She could see his fangs coming down, Jack couldn't wait to strike. Sharon told Jack that she discovered the killer was laying low out in the desert city of Palmdale.

She told Jack that she would radio in for back up once they hit the city limits. Jack advised her against it. Jack convinced Sharon that the two of them alone would suffice in taking down one unsuspecting criminal. Sharon reluctantly agreed, so it seemed.

"Jack don't cross me on my promotion," Sharon warned. "Or the ass whooping you got yesterday from whoever, will seem like child's play."

Jack wasn't concerned with a promotion for Sharon nor was he threatened by her. In fact, Jack was now planning to kill Sharon as soon as she led him to the killer. Jack was sure she had uncovered the truth. She had become a liability the moment she discovered his past.

Sharon pulled on the block, parking down the street from the house in question. She reached over opening the glove box and grabbing a pair of binoculars. She began spying the house. Sharon's head moved from side to side as she scanned the house for nearly two minutes before a sighting.

"Look! Upper level, back of the house," Sharon spoke, passing Jack the binoculars.

Jack zoomed in on the back of the house catching a glimpse of a big black man passing the window. Jack followed the man's movements towards the front of the house. Jack was finally able to get a good look of the man.

"My intel says he's in the house alone," Sharon added.

Jack scanned the bottom level of the house, there was no signs of life on the first floor. Jack placed the binoculars in the middle console of Sharon's car, grabbed his pistol and took the safety switch off.

"Let's go get this son of a bitch," Jack said, sliding out of the car first with his pistol in his hand.

Sharon followed Jack up the block along the houses with her gun in hand. They made it to the back of the house without being spotted. Sharon made quick work of the lock and the pair enter the house. Jack hand gestured Sharon to takes the stairs in front of the house, he would take the back stairway up.

Jack crept silently as he could up the stairs making every turn with gun pointed straight ahead. Jack landed on the top level inching slowly along the hallway. Sharon approached from the other end of the hall. Both Jack and Sharon could hear the television blaring loudly from the room in the middle of the hallway, Jack was two doors away.

Jack was passing the first door when he felt metal being forced against the side of his head.

"If you think you fast enough, go for it," A voice in the room spoke, offering an opportunity.

Jack looked straight ahead at Sharon who ducked off in the nearest room when she saw the pistol pushed against Jack's head. She peeked out to see Jack barely shaking his head from side to side advising her not to try anything. A hand came out, relieving Jack of his weapon. Another hand came out and Jack was snatched in the room.

"You looking for me cop," DA said, punching Jack to his knees.

"This place'll be crawling with cops any minute," Jack warned. "This'll be the only chance you have of escaping. You might want to take advantage of that opportunity."

Jack was confident Sharon would get the drop on this guy and he would be able to take care of them both as he had planned. Sharon turned the corner yelling freeze as she stood in the doorway aiming her pistol at DA.

"Looks like that opportunity just faded away son," Jack said, smiling and laughing. "Shoot this bastard Officer Brown."

"My pleasure sir," Sharon responded, moving in closer while still holding her aim on DA. "Drop the fucking weapon now!"

"Shoot this fucking piece of shit Brown," Jack hollered. Shoot his ass, shoot 'em now."

"If I was you, I'd watch where I was pointing that thing," DA advised. "You wouldn't want to shoot your superior on accident now would you?"

"No my love. I want to shoot his ass on purpose," Sharon said, lowering her weapon to Jack's chest level.

Jack instantly knew he had been set up. He frowned his mouth at the sight of Sharon.

"You double crossing bitch," Jack yelled. "You just fucked that promotion goodbye."

"Come here queen and cuff his ass up," DA directed.

Sharon walked over and slapped Jack in the mouth with her pistol. She and DA followed the tooth ejected from Jack's mouth in a rainbow hurl as it landed on the other side of the room.

"You bitch!" Jack screamed, wiping the blood from his mouth. "I'll kill you."

Sharon stood behind Jack, next to DA as she pulled her cuffs and prepared to hook him. Jack knew he would only get one opportunity to escape, he made his move.

Jack threw his weight backwards with his shoulder and elbow. The sudden force threw Sharon into DA and Jack was running out the door before either of them could react.

Jack turned out into the hallway colliding with some huge object and falling backwards, smacking the back of his head against the wooden floors. He shook it off to notice three more people staring down at him. Crafty grabbed Jack by his shirt collar, dragging him back in the room.

"Sit his dumb ass up," DA instructed, walking over and placing the handcuffs on Jack himself.

"Ok dumb ass. This is what I need you to do for me," DA said, pulling the detective's cell phone from its hip case. "I'm about to call your chief and you're going to tell him exactly what you see on the cards that my sister is holding."

"What makes you think I'm going to cooperate with you," Jack asked, defiantly.

Pockets walked over showing the before and after pictures of Jesse Adams. Jack glossed over the pictures and turned his head. He couldn't stomach it. Jack started throwing up.

"This is my handy work cop and as you can see I get a lot of enjoyment from my line of work," Pockets uttered. "Its gon' be my pleasure to work with you. You don't cooperate Jack and I promise to work with you real slowly."

Jack began to consider his options. He had none. It was either do as told or take his chances with the short psycho. Jack agreed to do as he was told.

DA placed the call putting the phone on speaker. The chief answered and Jack read from the cards as instructed.

"I'll see you there in a half of hour," the chief spoke, disconnecting the call.

"Alright let's finish up here and roll out," DA directed. "We have a king snake to kill."

Sharon walked over to DA and he gave her a gun and a head nod. Jack watched the exchange knowing his fate had just been sealed.

"Any last words cop," Pocket asked, giving Jack his last opportunity to pray for forgiveness.

Sharon interrupted any words Jack might have had, stepping in front and aiming her pistol at his head. Jack smiled, he didn't believe Sharon had it in her.

"Yeah I got some last words," Sharon said, cocking the hammer of the pistol back. "Fuck you! You racist pervert."

Sharon fired the first shot in the head of Jack. He fell backward with his eyes already closed. Jack was dead. Sharon emptied the rest of the shells into his body.

"I got a good feeling tomorrow will be a great day at work for you Sharon," Dana joked.

The crew cleaned up any evidence that would have been left and headed on their way to Malibu.

Chapter 16

Back Down Memory Lane

DA stood outside of Sharon's car leaning through the window. He was giving her final instructions on how to proceed with the chief of Police once he arrived.

"You cool baby," DA asked, kissing Sharon on the lips through the window.

"I'm good baby," Sharon spoke, assuring DA not to worry. "I can handle this with ease.

"Just keep him busy looking at the photographs or whatever," DA instructed. "We'll be pulling up right behind you exactly two minutes later. You remember the code?"

"DA she got it," Dana said, urging DA to let her go. "C'mon we wasting time."

"Go DA," Sharon added. "I got it."

DA stood staring down at Sharon. "Go ahead. I'll see you there and be careful."

DA understood how ruthless the chief was. Sharon had the most difficult job. One slip up by Sharon and the chief would shoot first and make up lies later.

Sharon pulled off racing down the stretch of Malibu's Pacific Coast Highway. She headed to a place called the Malibu Seafood restaurant. This is where the meeting with the chief of police would take place. Sharon pulled into the lot and backed her car in. She turned off her engine and waited patiently.

The restaurant was closed at this time of night. Sharon sat expecting no one but the chief to show. Sharon glanced down at her watch to check the time. It was five minutes until the meeting's scheduled time would arrive.

Sharon's wait lasted another two minutes before approaching head lights caught her attention. Sharon peered at the driver as he pulled closer. It was the chief.

The chief backed his Mercedes alongside Sharon's Dodge Charger and rolled his window down. Sharon did the same.

"Detective Brown, where in the hell is Detective Barnes at?" The chief yelled. "I don't have all fucking day."

"He should be along any minute sir," Sharon answered. "He said he wanted to be certain about something before he discussed it with you."

"What is this he's screaming about the cop killers?" The chief questioned. "He better have some damn good news."

"I have great news sir," Sharon said. "I have identified the cop killer."

"You have! And not Jack?" the chief questioned, cynically.

Chief Harris wasn't happy with that revelation. It showed on his face as he thought to himself, *who the fuck does this black bitch think she is*.

"That's right sir. I did and not Jack," Sharon reaffirmed, reading the chief's facial expressions.

"Are you sure we can make it stick," Chief Harris inquired. "This guy has been pretty smart up until now and we certainly don't need to look anymore unprofessional than this killer has already made us seem. What kind of evidence are we talking about here?"

Sharon held up a thick file for the chief to see.

"Motive, opportunity, forensics, every bit of evidence needed to send the bastard to death row," Sharon commented, sliding out of her car and walking over to the chief's car.

Sharon slid in the passenger's seat of the chief's Mercedes and slid into her all-star performance.

"His motive is, he blames cops for the death of his family," Sharon spoke. "He's a self-made multi-millionaire from an internet company, so that's your means and opportunity."

The chief listened as Sharon sold the story better than professional con man.

"This is a torn piece of shirt belonging to Detective Jesse Adams. I found this in a garage where I believe Adams was tortured and killed. I had it analyzed by forensics," Sharon said. "It came back positive for blood stains and was positively identified as blood belonging to Detective Adams."

Chief Harris took the small plastic baggie from Sharon, turning it from side to side. "So now we have time and location of death. Good work."

"We also have these photos that were found, taken by the perp," Sharon told. "I do advise you to be cautious. They're pictures of Detective Adams being tortured to death."

"The bastards took photos?" Chief Harris asked, enraged at the thought of this perpetrator's boldness.

"Unfortunately he did sir," Sharon replied, handing the pictures over to the chief.

The chief viewed every picture without blinking an eyelid.

"This perp can go fuck himself! Got it!" Chief Harris uttered. "He won't be seeing a court room anywhere here on earth!"

"No sir. He damn sure won't," Sharon replied, understanding the chief's insinuation. "He can always be killed while serving a high risk warrant. Obviously he's armed."

"What's this prick name?" The chief asked.

"Arrington. Darryl Arrington, the second sir," Sharon spoke. "He's the son of Darryl and Diane Arrington, two district attorney's that lost their lives in a fatal car accident some years ago."

"Yeah yeah yeah I remember the story," Chief Harris interrupted. "So junior wants to play in the big leagues. We'll have to make sure junior gets a nice going away party."

Chief Harris continued to view the pictures. He took his time studying each photo with a scrutinizing eye. The chief's concentration was broke with the introduction of bright headlights. Another vehicle pulled into the restaurant parking three feet from grill to grill with the chief's car. It was a black Jaguar.

"This must be Jack now," Sharon speculated, opening the door and stepping her feet out of the car.

"Hold on. Let's make sure it's Jack first," Chief Harris advised, pulling Sharon's arm and halting her movement. The chief pulled his gun from beneath his jacket and pulled back on the chamber.

Sharon looked at the chief and followed his lead, drawing her own weapon and waiting patiently.

The headlights were bright causing near temporary blindness for the chief and Sharon. The driver's door opened and a murky silhouette emerged. Chief Harris couldn't make out the person's identity but he could recognize a gun to his head.

"Gimme that!" Sharon yelled, snatching the gun from Chief Harris's hands and tossing it out the door. Sharon slapped the chief in his head with the pistol, screaming more commands. "Flash the lights!"

The chief was hesitant and Sharon pushed her gun into his head.

"Do it now! Flash the lights!" Sharon demanded.

"I guess you already know, you fuck yourself out of a retirement," Chief Harris responded, pulling the lever to flash the lights.

Sharon snatched the keys out of the ignition and place them in her shirt pocket.

"Out fat man!" Sharon ordered, exiting the vehicle herself.

DA stepped forward from the partial darkness. Sharon approached the other side the vehicle, gun still drawn on Chief Harris.

The chief remained calm as if he was in control of this event. DA walked over staring Chief Harris in the eyes, they both stood six foot three inches.

Crafty slid out of the passenger's door with a small white bag and walked over standing next to DA. Crafty nodded his head at DA.

Chief Harris looked at the two huge men with vengeance in their eyes. He knew with certainty they were going to kill him. At this point it was only speculation but the chief assumed Jack Barnes had to be dead. The chief's only chance of survival was to attempt an escape. As soon as the first opportunity presented itself, Chief Harris would take it.

Dana and Pockets slid out of the black Jaguar a second after Crafty.

"Aww that nigga dun' fucked up. That nigga dun' fucked up," Pockets harmonized, shaking Crafty and DA's hand. "What's up DA? So this the fool that killed y'all parents huh."

Pockets didn't say a word, he stared at the chief before throwing a combination punch. A left to his rib cage and a right to his chin. Chief Harris stumbled across his own feet, crashing his body against his car. "One of those was for me never meeting my in-laws, the other one was for my woman cracka ass."

"Pockets chill out man," DA demanded.

"My bad homie. That was for all of them nights I had to listen to my woman crying over not knowing her parents," Pockets told. "Shit pissed me off."

"It's understandable," DA confided. "We gon' squeeze a little time in for that."

Dana stood looking at the chief while he leaned against the car bleeding from the mouth.

"This just beginning for you," Dana warned. "You're gonna beg us for death."

"In your dreams little girl," Chief Harris replied.

"My dreams come true," Dana stated. "Your dumb ass is here with us now and I've been dreaming about this day for a good minute."

"You idiots will never get away with this," Chief Harris scolded.

The entire group burst out in laughter.

"I'm not sure but I believe every one of your officers said the same thing," DA teased.

"You idiots will never get away with this," Pockets repeated, mimicking the chief. "DA please let me have a moment with him."

Pockets glared at the chief.

"The picture of Jesse Adams is gon' look like a postcard, compared to what I'm gon' to do to you chief," Pockets threatened.

"Let's load his ass up and roll out," DA called out.

DA and Crafty loaded the chief into the passenger seat of his Mercedes. Crafty drove and DA sat behind the chief.

"Anything brave from you," DA cautioned, laying the silencer over the chief's shoulder. "And it'll be a quick, quiet ending for you," DA finished, pressing the pistol to the back of the chief's head.

Sharon and Dana drove in Sharon's Dodge and Pocket's followed in Dana's Jaguar. All three cars traveled closely along the road.

"Where are you taking me?" The chief asked.

"Back down memory lane," DA replied. "To where we became destined to have this meeting."

The chief looked on in confusion.

The caravan proceeded up the road. Sharon and Dana discussed the enjoyment they received from getting revenge. Both felt a weight had been released from their shoulder.

"Aww shit!" Sharon cried out, watching the chief's car swerving in and out of the lane. "Something's wrong!"

"Get next to 'em!" Dana screamed, as Sharon accelerated. "Get next to 'em!"

The women watched as the Mercedes nearly wrecked into the side of the cliff, swerved back out across both lanes of traffic and headed for the cliff again.

The chief figured if he was going to die, it minds well be on his own terms. Chief Harris leapt across the middle console, grabbing the wheel causing a struggle to ensue.

"Ahhh! Get this muthafucka DA! He trying to kill us all! Ahhh!" Crafty yelled, fighting for possession of the steering wheel as the car swerved about recklessly.

DA was thrown around in the back seat dropping his pistol. DA leapt over the seat and pounded the chief in the back and side of the head with powerful blows from his fist. "Let…go…mutha…fucka, let…go!"

The chief wasn't letting go. He was strong. His age meant nothing to his massive frame. He accepted DA's blows, defending off most with a high raised shoulder. This was a struggle for life and death.

Pockets saw the chief's car weaving in and out of traffic and Sharon closing in on the left side.

"Ahhh naw! This cracka in there tripping," Pockets said, flooring the Jaguar to the right side of the chief's Mercedes. "I told deez' niggas let Pockets have 'em! Naw day ain't wanna let Pockets have 'em!"

DA reached around the chief ensnaring his throat in a choke hold. DA attempted to pull the chief back over the seat but Chief Harris held onto the wheel firmly while kicking wildly.

Sharon pulled her Dodge to the left side while Pockets pulled to the right side. Sharon and Pockets smashed the vehicles on both sides of the chief's car to keep Crafty from crashing against the cliff or going over the other side.

"Aaahhhh!" Dana and Sharon yelled, as the Mercedes smacked against the Dodge bumping it towards the edge of the cliff.

The three vehicles screeched and smashed along the rode blocking both lanes. The three vehicle swerved in unison only separating to bang together again as they raced down the road in a blazing trail of sparks.

"Ahhh! We gon' die my nigg!" Crafty screamed, to the top of his lungs as the Mercedes played pinball with the two other vehicles. "Get this mutha…fucka man!"

"I'm trying!" DA screamed, struggling with the out of control chief.

"Oh shit! Pockets got this," Pockets roared, trying to lock the Jaguar against the Mercedes to avoid smashing against the rocks. "Aaah! Hold it steady Pockets, hold it steady."

The three vehicles were now locked side by side emitting a trail of sparks that lit the dark road as they careened ahead.

DA's choke hold was taking effect on the chief's oxygen. The chief's grip loosened as DA pulled his top half over the back seat. Sharon, Dana and Pockets noticed the chief being pulled in the back seat by DA. The chief's feet were dangling over the seat. All three cars slowed their speed.

"Oh lets hurry up and get his ass to this cliff," Crafty urged. "I'm so kicking this muthafucka's ass."

Crafty signaled for both cars to continue to the destination. They were four minutes away.

Crafty pulled in to the cliff area between the other two cars. Crafty hopped out, snatching the back door of the Mercedes open and yanking the chief out with so much force that Chief Harris landed like a board.

Crafty straddled his chest giving the unconscious chief so many right hand punches, the chief woke up kicking and screaming.

"Don't you ever do no shit like that again," Crafty warned, as he punched away.

"Sharon toss the cuffs here," DA instructed, hovering over Crafty as he continued to beat the shit out of the chief.

Dana and Pockets quickly jumped in stomping Chief Harris the fuck out.

"Cracka! You tried to…kill…Pockets," Pockets bawled, tap dancing around the chief's upper torso.

Dana took the time to practice punting footballs. She lined up, taking the five yard jog, professional NFL punters used and booted his testicles into another part of his body.

Chief Harris rolled over shrieking in pain.

DA and Sharon joined the ten toes down crew. All five individuals stomped the bellowing Chief Harris until he was unconscious again.

"Here let's get his ass in the driver's seat," DA commented, grabbing his right arm.

Crafty grabbed his left arm and the rest of the group helped to get the chief in his car. DA handcuffed the chief to the steering wheel and closed the door. He opened the back door, grabbing the white bag and his pistol that had fell in the commotion.

DA pulled two fifths of alcohol from the bag, undoing one. DA grabbed the unconscious face of Chief Harris, tilting his head back and forcing the contents down the chief's throat.

The chief came to life gasping for air like he was being water boarded. DA kept pouring it down his throat and soaking his body with it. Pockets walked over with the plastic gasoline jug and started drenching the inside of the chief's car with fuel.

DA covered the chief with the second bottle throwing them both in the passenger's seat. The chief pleaded to make a deal. He told of another scenario and another set of players who allegedly conspired to have the Arrington's killed. The chief swore it wasn't him who had their parents murdered and urged to let him help catch the real culprits.

No one in the group cared.

"In the same manner that you had my parents killed," DA started. "Today, you gon' experience death in the same fashion. This is where it all happened," DA continued, leaning on the chief's window while letting his head scan the area. "This is where you chief, had your cowards push my parents off this very cliff after they doused my father with alcohol."

"It wasn't me you moron," Chief Harris argued. "You haven't scratched the surface yet. At least I'll die knowing you idiots haven't accomplished anything."

Chief Harris began laughing aloud and hysterically. He was mocking the group for their incompetence as he called it.

"Can I get a last cigarette? Actually I can light it myself," Chief Harris laughed, making a joke of his situation. "You boys and girls know nothing about the Commission Meeting do you?"

The group sat quietly staring at one another. No one had heard of the commission meeting. Chief Harris scanned the faces of the group while he smiled.

"Yeah I didn't think so," Chief Harris teased, feeling he had one up on the group. "I guess you don't know about the police league either. I got evidence against both groups. How do you think I still made captain?"

"DA what he talking about?" Dana questioned.

"He just trying to save his ass baby girl," DA replied.

DA stepped to the back of the car with the rest of the group. Pockets leaned in through the passenger's door and put the car in neutral. Chief Harris begged and implored a mile a minute.

"Flame on!" Pockets notified, tossing the flaming piece of rag into the back seat.

Chief Harris squealed like a pig as the entire inside of the car engulfed quickly. His body jerked and flailed aimlessly handcuffed to the steering wheel. The chief's body had become a screaming ball of fire. The group could still hears the screams of Chief Harris as he burned alive inside the flaming vehicle falling to the rocks. The car crashed at the bottom of the cliff, exploding like a bomb and silencing all cries.

The group stood watching what looked like a bon fire so far down. DA put his arms around Dana. She understood the look. Their parents had finally been avenged…or had they?

COP KILLAS, JUSTICE SERVED D. MANN

www.ingramcontent.com/pod-product-compliance
Lightning Source LLC
Chambersburg PA
CBHW070020260626
47159CB00005B/1897